PLACES AND FACES

ADVENTURES WITH MILES

PLACES AND FACES

ADVENTURES WITH MILES

MILES CIGOLLE

SUNSTONE
PRESS
SANTA FE

Sunstone books may be purchased for educational, business, or sales promotional use.
For information please write: Special Markets Department, Sunstone Press,
P.O. Box 2321, Santa Fe, New Mexico 87504-2321.
Printed on acid-free paper

eBook: 978-1-61139-

LIBRARY OF CONGRESS CATALOGING IN PUBLICATION DATA

(ON FILE)

WWW.SUNSTONEPRESS.COM
SUNSTONE PRESS / POST OFFICE BOX 2321 / SANTA FE, NM 87504-2321 /USA
(505) 988-4418

DEDICATION

For my parents
Edward and Theresa

CONTENTS

PREFACE

Places and Faces is a fictionalized memoir based largely on real events and real people, over a seventy-year span, starting at the midpoint of the 20th century. It's the collection of fifty tales filled with longing and gratitude, which taken together define the events and milestones of my life. Of course names of people and places are changed. If you weren't there, it may sound like a distant dream. We were searching for new ways to love. I look back with pride: Stonewall, Gay Liberation, Gay Rights, the Party Years, AIDS caregivers, Same-Sex Marriage and Transgender Rights. We accomplished a lot.

Each phase had its notable places and faces. As memories, they were all indelible. This book touches on a few, some large, some small. Some serious, some fun. Did you see Calvin Klein's 1984 Underwear Campaign? He boldly proclaimed a proud new male sexuality in Times Square, using Bruce Weber's enormous illuminated ads featuring the Brazilian model Tom Hintnaus in revealing white briefs. Things would never be the same. It would be hailed as one of the "Ten Pictures that Changed America." Here's to some other places and faces I still cherish.

1

EDWARD'S ADOBE

It was a real adobe with one-foot-thick mud and straw walls, a round Kiva fireplace in the corner of the living room, round log viga ceilings and rough stone slate floors throughout. Decades later it would have an historic plaque proudly mounted on the stucco wall next to the front door. But for now, for Edward, it was just a comfortable home for his young family, a place where he wisely knew they would all be happy. The adobe was his great adventure, an outpost of safety, a thousand miles from tired LaSalle Illinois, the gloomy factory town dominated by an enormous Westclock factory with its towering smokestacks, where Edward's sisters toiled away for years. The adobe was his great escape, far away in the southwestern desert, under a canopy of enormous thunderclouds. It represented freedom, a new way of living.

The adobe was in a neighborhood with dozens of other adobes, shaded by giant cottonwoods with their gorgeous yellow leaves. Just a short walk to Albuquerque's Old Town with its Plaza oasis, its Mexican restaurants busy serving tourists, its art galleries and fine arts museum where Edward's wife Theresa hung out with her artist friends, Geneva and Helen, learning about art, the anchor of her life. She would inspire her four children to become artists themselves.

That first Christmas in 1953 was the most special. Me and my twin sister Melanie were just two-years-old. We didn't understand what was going on; we just watched in wonder. The entire neighborhood came alive around us. An enormous pile of fine sand was delivered to the middle of the street in front of Edward's adobe.

For weeks before Christmas Eve, Mel and I looked on in amazement as everyone carefully folded the small brown paper bags to be lovingly filled with votive candles and sand. Hundreds of luminarias. That afternoon before Christmas Eve, Edward was extra busy, carefully placing the bags in neat rows, outlining the adobe roof and walls, the sidewalks and curving garden paths. Finally, when it was dark and all the house lights were turned down, Edward lit the candles, slowly one-by-one.

It was a clear, perfectly still night, full of a thousand stars. Edward's young family, all bundled up, parted the adobe slowly and walked the sidewalks together holding hands in the crowd, softly singing their favorite carols. Edward, the giant, was in the middle, carefully holding Mel and I tightly in his arms. He looked down to my older sister and brother walking at his side. He was beaming with pride. He had somehow achieved all this on his own. It was a miracle really. It was the happiest moment of dear Edward's life.

2

THERESA'S STUDIO

Mother or artist, Theresa was pulled in two directions. She loved working with clay at the kitchen table, making things for the family in her sunny make-shift artist's studio. The young children would gather round to watch, never any trouble. They were always on their best behavior. Afterall, they adored her. To them, she was the greatest artist on earth, with her ceramic plates and bowls and ashtrays. They would marvel as she loaded up her ceramics kiln with plain colorless clay pots which the next day were astonishingly colorful creations. How did she do that? She was like a magician. She was their greatest teacher, patient and encouraging. Off the kitchen in the small mud room was her private studio where she worked alone afternoons when the children were playing in the portal. She was patiently working on a grand mosaic in four large panels made up of her tiny hand glazed tiles, each cut to fit perfectly, in watery shades of blues and greens and golds, an underwater world of exotic sea creatures drifting between aquatic plants. It would be her most ambitious work, ending up on the blank wall opposite the dining table. I always made sure I faced it during meals. I thought it was perfection, like nothing I'd ever seen before. And to think it was made by my mother. I was so proud.

The Albuquerque Art Club met bi-weekly at the Museum of Fine Arts off the Plaza. Terry rarely missed a meeting. They showed each other's work and sometimes revealed their secrets. Terry brought her bowls and plates, her smaller mosaic panels, sometimes a painting she was pleased with. They were mostly all women; there was only one regular man, Jerry. He made them all laugh. He was the one who told Terry she had real talent, she was a real artist, she should move to Santa Fe. Terry always blushed. She never told him she had a family. But alone later she secretly wondered what her life would have been like if she had never married, if she never had the children Edward expected. This question always haunted her as she sat at her small worktable staring into her blank white easel.

The twins, Mel and I, were standing at her doorway holding drawings from our afternoon play in the sunny portal. Mel held a fingerpainting of a little brown dog she had already named "Tommy." My abstract painting was a dense jumble of blues and reds like the stain glass windows I love in church. Terry praised each, as if they belonged in the local museum, especially my colorful altarpiece. "Miles, this is beautiful. May I keep it here by my side? It will give me inspiration." Then she stopped everything to give me a long hug. I had never felt her love so strongly before.

3

SIBLINGS'S PORTAL

The broad south side of Edward's adobe held its most special outdoor room, the long spacious porch, flooded with clear New Mexican sunlight. I loved its rough stone floor and long row of round wooden columns, like a row of telephone poles, which formed the traditional adobe portal that we all loved to play in. The narrow porch overlooked the shaded back yard with its high adobe walls and its thick soft floor of grass, where we'd lie on our backs at night looking up at the stars. In its center was Edward's red brick wishing well. Edward had constructed the covered well with its bird feeder to attract the hummingbirds he loved so much.

The backyard was a hidden secret world. Our grandmothers and aunts' houses back in LaSalle didn't have one of these playgrounds to enjoy when we visited each summer. We knew we had somehow lucked out; we'd hit the jackpot. We lived in heaven. This was our great outdoor playroom, where Edward and Terry relaxed with the Sunday paper, while I played with my siblings each day for hours. This was where we pursued our endless art projects under Terry's watchful gaze, both large and small, serious and silly, alone and together. Mel's messy finger paintings and Deb's delicious chocolate cream mud pies or Mark and I's futuristic toy houses made from cantilevered slabs of paving stone and tiny concrete bricks.

Terry kept an attentive eye as we took our afternoon naps on mats in the shade of the portal. I'd drift off, lost in the steady buzz of the summer cicadas. It was Terry's secret pride and joy, her children's private classroom with its treasured toys, where we played happily for hours. Terry understood that their fondest childhood memories could take seed here, to supply future nourishment in each to last a lifetime. Mark, Deb, Mel and I would each depart the secret garden within a few brief years. But time could not diminish the bonds of love formed within those adobe walls.

Edward's adobe still stands intact today. It looks much the same. The historic plaque by the front door was added by the proud current owners. They are an elder straight couple. When we knocked on the door they generously offered to give Abbey and I the full house tour. The interior was smaller than I recalled. The backyard was more lovely than I remembered. It's mature vegetation was now beautiful, lush with memories like the distant sound of children at play. An in-ground swimming pool had replaced Edward's red brick wishing well. These days on Christmas Eve, Abbey and I always take out time to walk by the house. The flickering luminarias leading up to the front door are still magical, soft and comforting. I stop a moment to relight an extinguished candle. In the darkness I can easily reconnect to Edward's beloved adobe. It lives on.

4

MENAUL AQUATIC
AND AN AFRICAN PRINCE

My parents had a thing for swimming pools. Back then, in the fifties, everyone did. My mother Terry must have seen pictures of Frank Sinatra's piano-shaped swimming pool in his new home in Palm Springs, California. She decided one day she would have one of those for her own family; and eventually she did just that. The house she designed in Albuquerque's Harvard Court would also have a piano-shaped swimming pool. That was fitting since both my parents adored Frank Sinatra.

Pools were always a part of our lives. Terry and Eddie settled for Menaul Aquatic until their dream house was built. It was a new pool club that we belonged to. On hot summer days it was our favorite routine. The kids were given swimming lessons. On our annual summer drives to LaSalle we always picked the motels with the coolest swimming pools for afternoon fun.

My earliest memories of male sexuality are from the Men's Showers at Menaul Aquatic. I must have been no older than five or six. I would stare at the naked men in the open shower stalls, walking around shamelessly, their cocks hanging out free, there buttocks tucked away into skimpy white towels. Some young trim guys were absolutely gorgeous. Just watching them made my head spin.

What made the greatest impression on me was the tall Black man. I always looked for him. I nicknamed him the African Prince. He was gorgeous, with the most beautiful dark black skin and contrasting white teeth. His skin was the color of bitter sweet chocolate, like the bars we'd buy from Lilac Chocolates on Christopher Street years later. It had a slight sheen, like the body builders I'd admire at the Chelsea. God was he beautiful. I stood frozen staring at him. He was tall and muscular. I was fixated on his big cock and giant butt. Naturally, I wanted to fondle them in the flesh, but I somehow restrained myself. I'd never seen anything like them. When he'd suds up, the snow-white soap would slide down his massive chest, across his round full butt cheeks, over his swollen cock and down to the tiled floor into a drain. I would have been content to watch him forever. He saw me and smiled. "Hey kid. Ready to hit the pool?" I was barely a kid. I wouldn't have my first wet dream for years to come. I hadn't a clue what sex was, but somehow, intuitively, I understood this was important, this was deep down a part of me. I would always cherish the memory of my African Prince.

5

ROSE GARDEN AND DR. KIRK

I inherited Terry's jungle, her unkept field of vegetation.
Her garden for wild roses, with pinks, tangerines and golden yellows.
What started out as a packet of seeds, soon turned into tender buds.
Towering over my head, their heavy blooms scented the air.

The garden was broad, but shallow, hugging the side of the house.
It was quiet and secluded, tucked up against a tall garden wall.
It was an explosion of vivid color, our own private Jackson Pollock.
With its thick petals and fleshy leaves, beware the nasty thorns.

At age six, I was crowned Terry's chief gardener, entrusted to care for it daily.
I was thrilled at the assignment, mama's little helper, tending her hidden joy.
It became my secret getaway, my favorite place to be alone.
Watering each plant with love, my daily communion with God.

Each morning I appeared with the scissors, looking for a few select blooms.
Gifts to give to our teachers, their thorny stems wrapped in aluminum foil.
That morning I was empty handed, when our gay neighbor suddenly appeared.
Dr. Kirk was tending to his roof air conditioner, he hadn't noticed me yet.

He was naked except for his red bikini, his athletic body on full display.
Seen from below, he looked like a God, suspended over Terry's rose garden.
I was fixated on his skimpy bikini, I'd never seen anything quite like it.
My head was pleasantly numb, I felt my first thrill of arousal.

He smiled looking down at me fondly, "Hey kid. I like your rose garden."
My mouth was dry, I couldn't speak, our brief encounter was over.
I was just a kid, but I already knew, my life was changed forever.
I dreamed of that red bikini for years, longing to unlock its secrets.

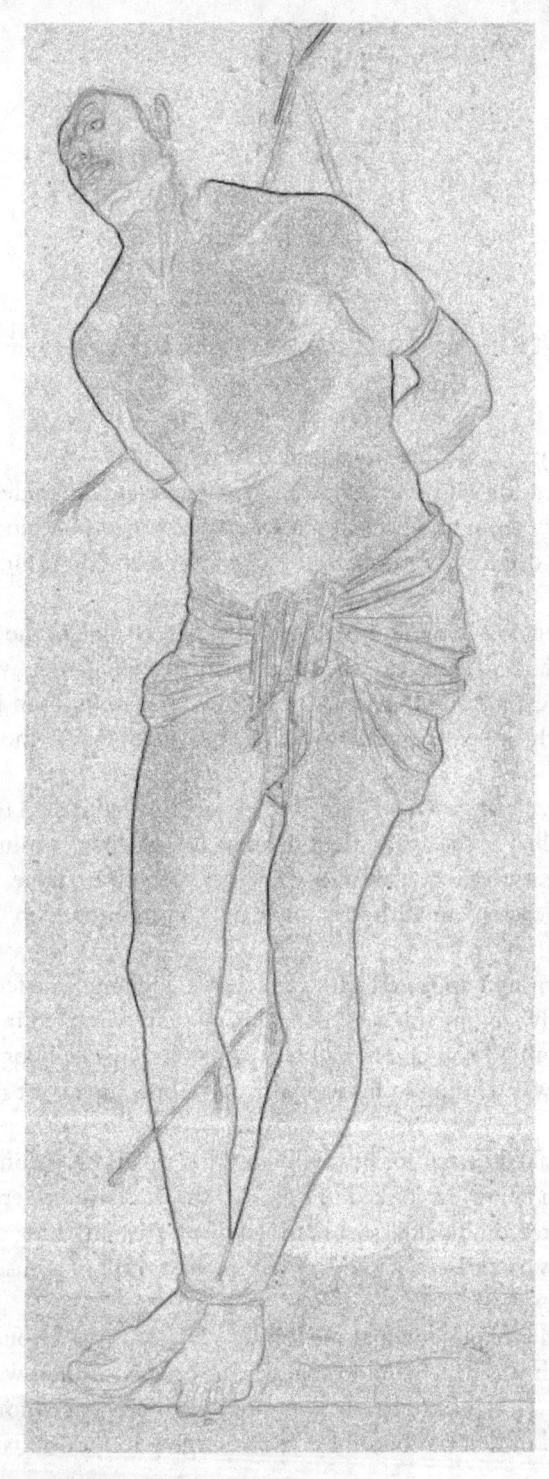

6

CAMP LASALLE AND SANDY

When I was sixteen my parents sent me to Camp LaSalle for the summer. It was a Catholic boy's camp run by Franciscan friars in the Pecos Mountains north of Albuquerque. I was surprised. None of my siblings had ever gone to camp. It felt odd, like a punishment, like I'd done something wrong. I guessed my parents knew I was turning into a homosexual and thought something had to be done to save me.

When they dropped me off on a warm Sunday afternoon, I was pleasantly surprised. The head brother gave me a warm welcoming hug and introduced me to a skinny boy named Sandy. Sandy and I would be doing work chores together. I was relieved I'd at least have a new friend. I liked Sandy right away. I thought he looked cool in his yellow baseball cap. As I hugged my parents in parting, I didn't know what to say. Terry shed a tear silently. Edward just muttered, "Be a good boy."

The camp was in a beautiful setting; gentle blue mountains all around with a golden stream running through the middle. Plus there were two unexpected surprises. They had a real leather workshop where Sandy and I could make things out of leather, and they had a stable with at least a dozen gentle horses. The horses had beautiful slightly shiny coats and the most wonderful big eyes I'd ever seen, dark brown and wet. I didn't feel safe riding them, but the brother let Sandy and me walk them in the paddock and rub their enormous heads. I think the horses liked us. We spent hours together in the shade of the giant cottonwoods. That's when I felt the happiest, with Sandy and my favorite horse Andy nearby.

That summer would turn out to be extra special. I learned something important about myself. I had always feared I would be all alone in the world because I had figured out I was probably a homosexual. Sandy showed me I was mistaken. Sandy soon became my new gay camp buddy. We were inseparable. The first thing he told me was he was a sissy. It was no big deal. He told me I was one too and that was just fine. It just meant we would be best friends. That made me extremely happy.

One lazy afternoon we were lying in the grass at the back of the paddock with Andy in the shade of a giant cottonwood. Sandy told me he'd seen my dick in the showers. He thought my dick was beautiful. He asked me if he could touch it. I said sure, why not. Afterwards, I told Sandy I also wanted to hold his cock. He said he would like that. He told me I could suck on his cock if I wanted to. Afterwards, he told me I did a great job. That made me extremely happy. It became our little secret. We'd meet regularly in the back paddock in the late afternoons to play with our private parts.

One of the older kids told me Brother Jeff and Brother Gene were secret "butt fuckers." I didn't know exactly what "butt fuckers" meant. Sandy told me he'd show me sometime out in the paddock. I will never forget that first time. Afterwards I felt blessed lying safely in Sandy's arms. My chest was all hot and sweaty. An enormous grin filled my face.

When I returned home I thanked my parents. They would never know just how important that summer would be for their son. I felt saved thanks to Sandy. Years later I would ask them why they sent me to Camp LaSalle. "We were worried about you. We could see in your face you were terribly sad; it broke our hearts. We loved you. We wanted to make you happy."

7

WELL'S MARKET
AND UNCLE CHARLIE

Well's Market was at the intersection of two old local trails, Rio Grande Boulevard and Indian School Road. My father Edward and his two older brothers, Charlie and Joe, together built and ran a grocery store there in the North Valley of Albuquerque. They had moved in the early 50's. My Uncle Charlie was a lunger, he had tuberculosis, and the Southwest had clean dry desert air that would save his life.

I worked summers in the store, mostly at Charlie's side, taking care of the dairy and produce, trimming, cleaning, arranging – the part us gays do naturally. It was my summer job through high school before going off to Cornell. I helped out in the store doing anything. I loved it. It was a chance to spend time with my father whom I hardly knew. I made a little money and I had real responsibilities. Soon I had the store in ship shape. Early Wednesday mornings we got the week's delivery from the main warehouse. Maybe a couple hundred cases to price and put on the shelves. My brother Mark and I tackled the mountain of cardboard boxes each week.

I noticed my Dad and my two uncles hardly spoke to each other. Strictly business. That seemed odd. I did practically everything with my three siblings, especially my two sisters. Wasn't it strange that Dad, Charlie and Joe never seemed to enjoy each other's company? I told myself I sure hope I don't end up like that.

The best part was working side-by-side with my Uncle Charlie.

He was in charge of the produce, dairy and butcher counter. He let me drive the store pick-up truck to make deliveries. Once I took a detour and got stuck in the desert sand on a dirt road. I felt awful. I'd let everyone down. But Charlie was terrific. He picked me up in a tow truck and never even asked me what had happened. He just hugged me and said, "Welcome back Miles, I guess we may need a bigger truck."

Charlie was my favorite uncle, my second father, my life-long friend. Charlie had no sons of his own. We shared unspoken secrets of boyhood. Charlie silently understood my budding sexuality. He had a secret stash of Playboy magazines he kept close tabs on by his lounge chair behind the butcher counter. Afternoons, when business was slow, Charlie relaxed in his chair, put up his feet, lit a cigar and cracked open this month's centerfold to study another pair of enormous tits. Charlie was pure hetero, plain and simple. The fact that his favorite nephew was a closet homo was not necessarily a problem. Now if I were asexual, uninterested in sex altogether, now that would be a serious problem. You see, Uncle Charlie, like me, loved sex period, hetero or homo, it was all good.

Charlie understood exactly what was going on. He was observant. No problem, he loved me and always made me feel welcome. The fact that he saw me show no interest in his Playboy pile, didn't really concern him. He knew my deeper interests lay elsewhere. So what did Charlie do? He threw me a life line. He added a new pile of magazines next to his treasured Playboys. This time they were all Playgirls. Wow! What an eyeful. Nude male bodies, sexy swimsuits, suggestive underwear ads, men with muscles and cocks. I tucked one under my work apron and locked myself away in the rear toilet room. Emerging sometime later with a grin on my face, Charlie spotted me and gave me a hug. "Let's go for a ride in the truck to the warehouse. I'll let you drive Miles." That was my Uncle Charlie. He had no problem with sex, period.

8

SPEECH CLASS AND MRS. ADAMS

She was a force of nature. Not only was she tall, large-boned and visually imposing, but her voice was powerful, like that of a Southern Baptist preacher, loud, strong and crystal clear. Mrs. Louisa May Adams was my speech teacher at Jefferson Junior High. She had a towering presence, reinforced by sturdy black high heels and a full head of curly dark hair.

I was just fourteen, and I loved her. Here I was, this shy quiet awkward kid and along comes Mrs. Adams, the Hurricane. She'd change all that. She'd instill in me the confidence to speak before a crowd with poise, courage and emotion. How thrilling. She pulled me out of my shell and introduced me to the wonderful worlds of great literature and poetry. Mrs. Adams lit the spark that ultimately turned me into an avid writer.

I really can't recall how it came about. Was it another of Terry's ploys to make me tough, more masculine, less of a sissy? Or, was I just luckily drawn to it, on my own? Either way, what a happy accident. We met several times a week in Mrs. Adams' second-floor classroom, next to the noisy Band Room. Mrs. Adams didn't mind the occasional intrusion of marching band music. She might have even welcomed the outside noise as competition, to help train her young students in the rudiments of public speaking: proper posture, breathing, diction, projection and dramatization. I loved to study her large expressive lips carefully shaping each vowel lovingly, like an oyster polishing the perfect pearl.

But certainly, the best part of it all, was the introduction to the world of poetry. That's basically all we did; stand up in front of the class and recite poetry or prose with expression, with emotion, with heart-felt feeling. We were each asked to select a work on our own, something we felt a connection to personally. It was really something. I immediately understood why poetry is meant to be read aloud with facial expression. It must engage our whole body, it must come out of your soul if it is to come to life. So many great treasures we explored together. It was like a shared communion.

I read aloud passages from Walt Whitman's *Leaves of Grass*. By that point I had figured out that he was a homosexual like me. He was a secret hero. I selected this passage from Whitman's epic homoerotic poem "Song of Myself."

"I mind how once we lay such a transparent summer morning,
How you settled your head athwart my hips and gently turn'd over upon me,
And parted the shirt from my bosom-bone, and plunged your tongue to my
*   bare-stript heart,*
And reach'd till you felt my beard, and reach'd till you held my feet."

What a tremendous gift to a shy young closeted man. Thank you, Louisa May, for unlatching the door and welcoming me into the exciting worlds of words and feelings and speech.

9

TERRY AND EDDIE'S DREAM HOUSE

We moved into Harvard Court in Albuquerque's Pill Hill when I was just a freshman at Jefferson Junior High. It was my parent's dream house, custom-designed primarily by my mother. Terry should have been an architect. She had "good taste," plus she had the natural talent to manipulate space like a professional. Her two sons, me and my older brother Mark, became architects instead. Terry had to settle for being the weekend artist, that and a reluctant housewife.

The house was inspired by Edward and Terry's love of Japanese architecture and Japanese rock gardens adored from afar. They would never see that exotic world first hand. In fact, it was not until decades later that Abbey and I made the necessary pilgrimage to Kyoto to close the Japanese circle. The Harvard Court house was a classic Japanese house concept, a horizontal low-slung wooden structure built around three open-air courtyards. Edward turned the central courtyard into a Japanese water garden with tiered pools. I loved the sound of cascading water that filled the whole house. The carefully composed landscape of stepping stones and pine trees with giant boulders asleep like beasts was Edward's doing. Terry designed the unique in-ground swimming pool shaped like a glacial pond. Inside, the exposed beam cathedral ceilings, polished brick floors and rough stone fireplaces reflected Terry's sophisticated taste. The comfortable well-designed house was in another world from the family's first modest adobe home.

It was heaven while it lasted, only six or seven brief years, before the four kids all went off to college, to Princeton, Brown, Cornell and Colorado, never to return to Albuquerque. For a few years thereafter my parents lived in the house alone. It must have been difficult walking by those empty children's bedrooms day after day. The house is still largely intact today sixty years later. We drive by it occasionally. Two childless physicists from Sandia Labs live there now. Little do they know the exuberant life that once filled these now empty rooms, those children's faces full of laughter and love.

10

SIBLEY HALL AND CODY

When I arrived on the Cornell campus for the first time in the fall of 1969 I knew absolutely no one; Sibley Hall was to be my new home full of strangers. Dating back to 1870, the three-story stone building had a white central library dome easy to spot from the Arts Quad. I loved the College's compactness, it promised future friendships. The entire College of Architecture, Art and Planning fit neatly within her walls. Besides our two-level library under the dome, it contained the Dean's Office, the College Gallery, the Green Dragon Café, all the faculty offices plus our classrooms and the spacious Design Studios where we spent endless hours working and clowning around. I was slowly making a couple of new friends, but it wasn't easy. Still I had hope; for even the grad students were housed there with their tales of upper-class adventure.

First day of class was a traditional rite of passage. Simple I thought. They want to take a picture of the incoming freshman class. The sixty of us arranged ourselves on the exterior steps into Sibley Hall's main entrance overlooking the Arts Quad. "Smile!" Oops! Down comes fifty gallons of water from the roof directly over us, courtesy of the upper classmen.

Every year on St. Patrick's Day in March the first-year architecture students created an enormous paper-mâché dragon that made its way across campus interrupting lectures and library study. "Dragon Day" ended with the dragon consumed by a huge bonfire on the Arts Quad. One classmate came dressed as a Native American Indian, performing a dance ritual around the fire. I joined others up for a night of debauchery at our Beaux-Arts Ball. But the gay students were too closeted to bring same-sex dates.

Second year at Cornell, I had a crush on my fellow classmate Cody. It was a thankless obsession. He was short, with a sexy Italian stride. He wore painter's work overalls that drove me crazy. He'd pose in them for my benefit. He liked to humiliate me. "Miles is a closet queen. He's still a virgin." He belittled my tender love, put down my budding homosexuality. He was the sophisticated bisexual touting superiority with both a boyfriend and a girlfriend in tow at the same time. I was just a lonely closeted homo. How could I compete with Mr. Cool?

I pinned all hope on Cody's sense of humanity, his generosity, his love. I was dead wrong. He showed me none of that. Instead he made me hate him. That was the most awful. I'd never hated anyone other than the playground bully Kevin. Cody and Kevin were the same monster. I was a fool to love Cody. He taught me love's first painful lesson - beware the fickle lover; his face is cruel and deceitful.

11

CORNELL PLANTATIONS AND UNCH

It was our slice of heaven. The Cornell campus was nestled between two spectacular gorges with their stone staircases, footpaths and waterfalls. Coming from the desert of New Mexico I was in constant awe. My classmates and I spent sunny fall afternoons skinny dipping in the pools, napping on slate slabs on our towels, flaunting our youthful bodies like Greek gods and goddesses. It wasn't sexual in the least bit. We were far too green for that. We were all simply searching for new friendship, comradery, a new trust. Sex would come later. This was the end of adolescence, the last echoes of childhood.

With over five hundred acres of rolling green hills, gardens and nature areas, the Cornell Plantations were always a draw. As new architecture students it was our favorite walking destination, with our cameras around our necks, playing Edward Weston or Minor White, searching for the truth. The perfect way to spend a spring afternoon. Quiet and at peace. Sharing our most private secrets. At the far end of our trajectory, we discovered an overgrown field complete with brown and white dairy cows grazing around a dozen massive concrete sculptures, Corbusian-inspired sentinels. These towering monoliths were the gift of our predecessors, the inspired creation of another class of architecture students from a decade before us. I was deeply impressed.

On other days Unch would take me on a leisurely drive with a couple of sandwiches and a bottle of spring water. Just the two of us. I suspect he had vague hopes of seducing me out in the open. I was one of the closeted homosexuals in our class. I wish he'd been less polite. He should have raped me with full force right there on the grass, ripped open my blue jeans and devoured my virgin cock whole. I didn't give poor Unch the slightest opening. I was locked up in my shell. Instead, we'd sit together on the soft grass in the shade of giant oaks, looking up at clouds, talking about nothing, avoiding the obvious. Unch was so handsome, always dressed to the nines. My eyes feasted on his sexy tight trousers, the plump center package just waiting to be neatly unwrapped. Ah, what a wasted opportunity. Instead, we focused on his other pride and joy close by, his gorgeous orange Porsche, his other macho sex machine, as beguiling as Unch's hidden hardon. He liked to drive both real slow, the car and the cock, to milk each throttle to the max, so as to not disturb the tranquil setting. That was Unch, always the gentleman.

Why did I hold myself back? Was Terry looking over my shoulder? Stupid fool, I missed a shot at heaven. I wouldn't appreciate Unch fully until years later, much too late, by that time he was captive to AIDS.

My roommate Rich was my guardian angel, always looking over my shoulder, ready to lend a hand, to show me the way. Ironically, he died of AIDS and I survived for more than thirty-five years. I still miss him. Others were too quick to dismiss Rich as unsophisticated, a mama's boy, a sissy, a fag. Rich could care less. His face was full of courage and kindness.

12

MORRIE'S AND DEREK

Derek was a townie in his thirties when I met him. Derek and Rich were regulars at Morrie's, Ithaca's only gay bar. Derek was always on the lookout for fresh "chicken." Rich explained. Derek was what's known in the gay world as a "chicken hawk," an older gay man who's looking for an attractive younger male, or a "chicken," for queer sex. I knew none of this lingo; I was so naïve at the time. Derek was a tall skinny Black man with a short Afro. He had a handsome face, sapphire blue eyes and gorgeous white teeth. He took very good care of himself. Not an ounce of fat. In his prime he must have been a knock out.

Rich told me Derek owned his own local catering business. He operated it out of a large kitchen in a rundown house he owned downtown in the flats. He catered small events at Cornell. It provided a modest income, enough to cover his bar tab. He gave Rich an open invitation to work anytime as a waiter and earn a little extra cash on the side. That first night after I met Derek in Morrie's, Derek extended the same offer to me. I guess I got the thumbs up; he liked me.

I was quickly turning into a Morrie's regular myself, a not-so-shy bar fly. I was just a voyeur watching from the sidelines, hovering around Rich. I never went home with anybody. Derek always made a fuss over me, buying me beers, serenading me with his corny embellished version of Barbra Streisand singing Memories on the jukebox. I sometimes wished he'd just leave me alone. But I had to admit, he was nice to look at in his tight pressed chinos. I was sure he was hiding a big Black dick.

Rich kept telling me to relax and circulate, talk to guys who were my type. I didn't even know what my type was. Rich said I'd never meet anyone just standing around feeling sorry for myself. So, with Rich's encouragement, I decided to lighten up. The next day I bought a new pair of skin-tight faded button-fly Levi's. But the only one who noticed my sexy new jeans was Derek. "Miles, you look super-hot tonight. Are those new jeans? Very nice Miles. It's closing time. Let's go to my place. I'll give you a nice massage. My van is right out front." I don't know why I gave in so easily that night. I guess I was horny. I wanted to shed my virginity, to finally come of age. I figured Derek was a stud and he was crazy about me for some reason. I needed an education.

The house was nothing special; your basic Ithaca 2-story house. Derek took us around to the back porch, stopping to grab a heavy rug from the clothes line. He opened the porch door and tossed the rug down in the middle of the kitchen. "Miles, get us two beers from the refrigerator. I'm thirsty." As I turned to open the refrigerator door, I felt his strong hands from behind on my shoulders forcing me down to the floor onto the rug. He was stronger than me. I was helpless.

"Relax Miles. I love you, but I have to teach you a lesson. You should watch out where you wear your skin-tight Levi's. They get a guy like me a little overexcited." With one hand tight on my bare butt he had me pinned to the floor. He gave himself a thick wad of saliva in his free hand and then took out his fully erect cock. Then with a single thrust, he fucked my white virgin ass. The pain was excruciating. I'd never been really butt-fucked before except by Sandy at camp. That didn't count. Sandy was mostly just pretending. But with Derek it was the real thing, 100%, and his cock was extra-large. He spared me nothing. He treated me like a grown man. I was getting the education I wanted.

Then Derek paused for a very long time. He started humming "Memories" from Morie's jukebox. He eventually commenced the age-old ritual of queer butt sex. I took deep breaths like Derek told me to. The pain slowly receded. To my astonishment the pain was replaced by the deep sensation of anal pleasure. "There Miles buddy, you're doing great. You have a beautiful butt. Relax, we're on the ocean together." Derek kissed the back of my neck as he gently butt-fucked me. "Please don't stop Derek. Make love to me like a real gay man, I don't want to be a sissy virgin." Derek smiled as he resumed the ancient sex ritual; the same one Emperor Hadrian performed with his beloved Antinous. Derek started humming Memories once again as his hardon returned with new vigor. "Miles, I'm going to crown you a man tonight." So I surrendered myself completely to Derek. I could finally disappear. I felt Derek's powerful lungs over me gently moving with each breath, with each full thrust of his mighty cock. His beautiful giant hands cradled my head off the floor. At last, Derek and I were one. That night Derek gave me my manhood. It was a one-night stand.

13

GREEN DRAGON AND TIM

Tim was in the class behind me in Cornell's College of Architecture, Art and Planning. I'd first seen him in the Green Dragon, the college café in the partial basement of Sibley Hall under the white dome of the Fine Arts Library. It was a lively place, popular with architecture undergrads, post grads and young faculty. I hung out there to take in the people, especially guys like Tim. I wasn't even out yet, but I told myself I could always make an exemption for Tim, but he never paid me any attention.

That morning I was in luck. Tim appeared. As usual he sat alone in a corner reading his paperback novel. This morning it would be Nabokov's Lolita with a green cover. Tim was a carefully studied work of art, a real cock-tease. He was terribly sexy in a casual relaxed-sort-of way, with his paint-splattered sneakers up on the low slate table top, seated in a black director's chair, leaning back in the chair on two legs against the exposed brick wall. He looked very laid back indeed, with his blue paper coffee cup balanced on his knee, dressed in frayed blue jeans, a ripped white t-shirt and outrageous pink socks. His light brown hair was long, almost to his shoulders, not terribly well kept. He looked like a hippie without the tie-dye, or a bohemian artist taking a break from his painting studio upstairs, an intellectual for sure.

I couldn't stop staring at him. He radiated an aura of sex that left me light headed. When he got up to leave, I saw clearly that he was tall and lanky like Peter Fonda in "Easy Rider." I'd just seen that movie last night. I thought Peter would make the perfect lover. I realized Tim would as well. He glanced my way, walked slowly past me and then he paused. That's when it happened.

He delivered the slightest smile, a Mona Lisa smile, meant only for me. It was intensely erotic. As he slowly left the room, to start up the open stairwell, he looked back once for another look. Our eyes met. As he sashayed slowly up the stairs, I was completely fixated on his trim slinky backside, his sexy ass, his long dangling arms, his bouncy shiny hair. Then he suddenly stopped and turned around, so I could take in his whole front side from below, the faded jeans frayed white at the pockets, the crotch with its pale button fly, his trim waistline without a belt, the white wrinkled t-shirt. And most striking of all, against the t-shirt, was a thin gold chain necklace, with a single dangling gold ring, a man's wedding ring. He stood still for just a second, again just for me, before resuming his climb, two steps at a time, disappearing as suddenly as he had arrived. That was Tim. He was a butterfly, always ready to sample the next garden. You couldn't help but love him. His open and loving face. He was our gay flower child, the sleepy hippie with free love for everyone.

14

EDGECLIFF AND DAVID

It was an Arts and Crafts house that had everything—a quiet secluded location, an exterior straight out of a children's storybook, a romantic cozy interior with a wood-burning fireplace and the most spectacular view in all of Ithaca. It sat on the edge of the gorge cliff wall, overlooking the city lights of Ithaca far below. Architecture students had occupied the house for decades. They felt entitled. That seemed fair enough. It's romantic setting spoke to them more deeply than the other students. A graduating architect would pass their room on to some lucky AAP underclassmen, sort of an in-house lottery.

The cock tease Tim from the Green Dragon was one of the lucky ones. He lived there with a boyfriend. Well, not exactly, Tim's lover David was the Associate Dean of the Cornell Law School. David was easily twice Tim's age. Tim and David had the top floor to themselves. Generally they kept a very low profile.

I met David at one of their rare house parties. Everyone always wanted to see the view at night. I showed up alone in my leather jacket. I was feeling sexy. This was well before I met Jim. David had snow white hair; he was extremely handsome; he must have worked out every day. David obviously adored Tim, always at his side though Tim seemed less appreciative of David. Tim was still a kid. He had no idea how good he had it. I laughingly told David to drop this ditsy Tim and get a more mature boyfriend like me.

"I'm always looking for my man. Think you can handle me?" David laughed, but he took down my number anyway.

Sure enough, David called me up the following week. He asked me if I'd like to work out with him. He'd really enjoy having a gym buddy to keep him motivated. He said Tim never uses the gym. "It's so boring." I said sure, knowing full well it could only end in trouble. But I didn't care. I was lonely. I was practically a virgin and I was really turned on by David. I couldn't wait until we hit the steam room. We had a one-month fling. David was a passionate lover.

When Tim found out, David asked me to cool it for a while. No problem, I was leaving Ithaca for the summer. I was enrolled in Cornell's AAP summer program in Florence. Our parting was bitter sweet. I really loved David, but I knew David would never leave Tim. When I returned to Ithaca that fall, I finally came out for good and met Jim within a month. For the next nine years Jim and I were inseparable.

15

GALLERIA DELL'ACCADEMIA AND DAVID

It's totally outrageous. Completely over the top. I'm talking about Michelangelo's marble statue of the nude youth David, of David and Goliath fame, probably the most famous statue of all time. Everybody is told the story in art history class of how 26-year-old Michelangelo took a narrow block of rejected Carrara marble to carve by hand his 17-foot-tall Renaissance masterpiece. Scholars have written volumes on David's twisted contrapposto pose which looks like David is about to move, his unusually large head and right hand, his intense stare ready for battle. All this is true and much more, but when I first saw David in Florence's elegant Galleria dell'Accademia, standing alone on a high pedestal under a dome, all I saw was one very sexy stud, the perfect sex partner.

I'm sorry, but David simply reeks of sex. And in case you didn't know it, Michelangelo was gay. You can't tell me that at age twenty-six with Italian testosterone pulsing through his veins, that Michelangelo wasn't making love to David as he slowly released this Adonis from the stone. Each curve of every individual muscle is lovingly expressed. Looking at him, I want to caress his massive chest and abdomen of tight hard muscles, to trace his long regal neck up to his powerful athletic face, to feel my fingers comb through his thick curly hair.

He's a sex God. The ultimate "gym bod." David's much admired bubble butt is every gay man's dream, leaving us all with aching hardons. Only David's genitals are too small, out of scale with the rest of his body. Michelangelo knowingly leaves that important detail to each viewer's imagination. David is the body we all secretly lust after, standing nude on a pedestal, confident and proud.

The grand exhibition hall in front of David is lined with Michelangelo's half finished "Slaves." Each is emerging slowly, painfully, from its huge block of rough stone, their facial features undefined as if in a dream. These late unfinished works by the Florentine master perfectly compliment the youthful David. Looking at them I feel Michelangelo's exhaustion with life, perhaps his struggle to continue, his self-doubt, his humanity.

That summer was my first of many future visits with David and the Slaves. At the time I was just twenty-two years old, still firmly locked in my safe closet, afraid of my own sexuality. This first encounter with David would change all that. I would finally come out when I returned to Cornell that fall. I can thank David and dear Michelangelo for that.

16

LAVENDER HILL AND STANLEY

I met Stanley at my first gay dance at Cornell. It was held in the soaring neo-Gothic Memorial Room inside Willard Straight Hall. I was impressed. They gave us dancing queens the best room on campus. Stanley was a groovy dancer and gentle hippie. He was also a Cornell PhD grad student. Super nice. Stanley mentioned he lived in Lavender Hill. When I heard that my ears pricked up. I wanted to hear all about it.

Lavender Hill was pretty wild. It was the first LGBT commune in the country, exclusively for gay men and lesbians living together. Totally rural. Lavender Hill was on 80 acres, 15 miles south of Ithaca. The hedonist lifestyle was a trip. There was definitely lots of sex and the stretching of social norms. A certain amount of gender fucking; masculine men wearing ladies' dresses, that sort of thing. Plus some drug exploration, lots of music, singing and parties. There were sex orgies or love fests as they preferred to call them. They just happened naturally.

When I heard that, I asked Stanley if I could come to one of the Lavender Hill love fests. I've always thought hippies were really sexy in their tie-dye drag and their groovy bell bottoms. The Donovan look. I just wanted to spend quality time with those cute hippie guys. I knew I could learn a thing or two from them. They were all so beautiful.

Stanley told me the commune was closed to guests when it

comes to love fests. I could respect that. They were a family. If I suddenly showed up, it could upset the balance. When I suggested an outdoor orgy in the woods Stanley said sure, no one would even notice given their eighty acres.

Of course the outdoor male love fest was a big success. Eleven horny guys made sure of that. Stanley brought six guys from the commune who were all super cute and totally uninhibited. Everyone had a great time. Stanley was weighing the idea of a repeat performance in a month or two. Rich thought we should let things cool off for a while. We wouldn't want to cause any trouble down at Lavender Hill.

17

DEWITT MANSION AND JIM

It was an Ithaca three-story red brick Victorian pile with turrets, gargoyles and stain-glass windows. I was living there on the second floor. My buddy Rich lived downstairs with Jason and Jason's girlfriend Tina. Two cool Cornell gay-rights activists also lived on the ground floor, Jimmy and Jake. They gave wild parties for the cute college boys, a source of fresh cock for Jimmy who was always on the prowl. That's how I came out. Jimmy locked us inside his bedroom and showed me the world of queer sex, nonstop in a single night.

No wonder the house caught on fire. It was a hotbed of queer sex. Within a month of coming out I met Jim at Morrie's, the local gay bar. We were fucking in his bed after dinner when we heard several fire trucks racing down Seneca Street. It was the DeWitt Mansion a block away. The flames were as high as the trees. A student hot plate caught fire on the third floor causing a major fire that burned off the top floor. The mansion was temporarily condemned.

So, sooner than expected, I moved into Jim's basement apartment. I was thrilled. Within a month of coming out I was living full-time with the man of my dreams. Everything was happening too fast.

Jim was my first idol. More than a lover, he was the center of my world. My constant companion, he was my Guru and Savior. Jim was nine years older, a college professor, a future children's book editor. We would live together in New York City for nearly a decade in domestic bliss, or so it seemed on the surface. Jim spared me the tawdry side of coming out in the Big Apple, the lies, the dishonest tricks, the cheesy betrayals you hear about. But he also robbed me of my sexual debut, my secret lusts, my deepest desires. I was a horny eighteen-year-old eager to get my rocks off. Jim was more interested in his evening martini.

We each inadvertently extinguished the other. Slow suffocations. When I checked out on a solo winter vacation to Venice, Jim grabbed the opportunity and flew the coop first. I was devastated, or was I? I couldn't wait to hit the saunas and backrooms, the raunchy anonymous sex clubs. I was making up for a lost decade. Face to face with being alone again, I said, "No problem. I'm tough, I can take it." Only years later did I start to understand what had happened with Jim. I never saw Jim clearly from the start. He was my illusion, my dream.

AIDS dealt us an unfair hand. Within three years of our break-up, Jim and his new husband Philip would both die as early victims of that dreaded disease. My hope of retaining a core friendship with Jim and Philip for life was crushed forever.

18

DEWITT BUILDING AND DANNY

It was Ithaca's main old high school. A red brick pile. In 1972 a smart local architect bought it from the city for ten dollars and did a gut renovation turning it into slick modern apartments. My buddy Rich and I grabbed a two-bedroom. We liked living off-campus, away from our neurotic closeted classmates. Rich was out, having a ball screwing with the out-of-control townies. I had just met Jim and our new friend Bob appeared ready to take the homo plunge. It was an exciting time. We were busy redefining ourselves.

Our apartment was on the top floor, two floors directly above Moosewood, the soon to be world-famous vegetarian and vegan restaurant. It was owned by the entire restaurant staff, the Moosewood Collective, a hippie commune outside of Ithaca called Lavender Hill. They were creative and talented, as well as terribly sexy, especially when they took their aprons off. Bob, Rich, Jim and I started a weekly tradition of relaxed mid-week lunches getting to know the cute waiters. Occasionally lunch segued into an afternoon orgy upstairs on giant pillows on our apartment floor. Townies sure knew how to have fun. It was a quick education. A month later I would finally come out.

Every day around four in the afternoon the hippie drummers arrived in DeWitt Park with their massive bongo drums. A colorful mix of tie-dyed tee shirts and cotton dresses, Indian print skirts and Berkenstock sandals. The men all wore loose billowing trousers that looked more like sexy pajama bottoms. They had shoulder length hair or even longer down to their pretty asses, some braided, mostly not. African skull caps and colorful bead jewelry were popular. It wasn't easy telling apart the gay men from the lesbians, everyone looked androgynous, yet still sexy, as if any type of intimacy was welcomed. These were Ithaca's hippies, who met every late afternoon to worship the setting sun with their pagan drums before heading over to Moosewood for a shared vegan feast.

The hippies were pretty much everywhere. Nobody hassled them. I started befriending them. I loved their gentle faces. I'd settle in on the grass in front listening to the drums. I was in heaven. My whole head would feel numb. Sometimes I'd drift off smelling the pot. I got hooked. The drum sessions became my favorite daily routine. I was there every afternoon at three-thirty. I always left them five dollars in the kettle. I eventually learned a few of their first names, like cute Kevin, friendly Jonathan and sexy Danny, especially sexy Danny whose white cotton pantaloons looked like a giant diaper concealing his precious cock.

Danny must have figured out I had the hots for him. It was pretty obvious. I always sat down near him and paid him constant attention. Just being near him made my head buzz. My loneliness lifted. After a few weeks Danny sat down next to me during a break and offered me a drag on his joint. It was my first grass. I'd always declined joints when they were passed around in college. This was different. It wasn't about getting high. It was about getting closer to Danny. Danny was so cool with his relaxed sexy smile. He told me a few dirty gay jokes and got me laughing. Out of the blue he asked me if I'd like a blowjob after the drum session. I blushed. "Of course, are you kidding? How much do you charge?" He laughed. These hippies are into free love.

19

CORNELL TEAROOM AND RICH

My third year at Cornell I mustered all my courage to venture inside the infamous tearoom in Cornell's Student Union. Located in the bowels of Willard Straight Hall, how ironic that a building which looked like a proper Gothic cathedral on the outside, actually housed a den of the queerest perversion. I was long overdue for an introduction. My classmate Rich had told me all about it. Rich was already a regular, more like a nocturnal addict actually. Like clockwork, Rich would show up every evening at ten o'clock sharp for an easy hookup at the line of urinals on his way home.

The tearoom was in a perfect location off a deserted corridor in the sub subbasement. Distant footsteps were always audible from the stone floor. Plus, the posted lookout knew all the regulars by sight, so there was never any trouble. When I showed up on my first visit with Rich as my trusted guide, the lookout gave me a long once over, then a warm "Welcome Gents" as he opened the door for us. Once inside, the odor of used poppers made my head spin. Inside were a dozen guys going at it in full tilt. It truly was a cross section of the gay community from wire-rimmed John Lennon hippies to Ivy League nerds in their faded chinos and navy blazers. It was strictly an oral scene, popular with cute junior faculty and horny grad students who gladly serviced them. Plus an endless stream of curious under grads, all ripe and willing, who often turned out to be the most active of all. No one ever spoke a word; just soft moans of deepest pleasure. Guys were always patient and polite. The butch guy in biker leather immediately caught my full attention. He motioned me over for my first tearoom blowjob. I was in heaven.

Rich was a mama's boy. His mother sent him a letter every day from Alton, a suburb of St. Louis, keeping Rich up to date on the local gossip back home. On my cross-country drive third year in the VW bug, I picked up Rich in Alton. His mom welcomed me into her tidy home as a second son. We stayed in touch for years. A decade later we would meet again, this time in a peaceful Alton cemetery. It was a much sadder occasion. Our faces had lost their glow. Rich had died of AIDS.

20

REMSEN STREET AND WINDOW DRESSING

Before Jim and I moved there from Ithaca, I never realized just how gay-friendly Brooklyn Heights actually was. Sure, it had a tired old piano bar on Montague Street for the older crowd with their hair pieces and gold jewelry. Plus everybody knows the Brooklyn Promenade is a famous gay cruising area. I guess I was so wrapped up in blissful monogamy with Jim that I was blind to it at first. But just look out the window onto pretty Remsen Street. I started to notice there's a lot more going on than just dog walking. Cute young guys were loitering on the sidewalks in their leather jackets, lounging in the sunlight on the brownstone stoops, showing off the goods in their tight revealing trousers as they stood up to stretch and preen. It went on all day and night. Just pay attention.

I started noticing one particularly hot number on Remsen Street, a leather queen in his worn motorcycle jacket, who always wore tattered jeans with no belt and a tight white tee. I didn't mention him to Jim. Jim wouldn't understand. He didn't crave raunchy anonymous sex like I did. I assumed he was simply too old. One day I saw the guy enter # 70 directly across the street from our building. Perfect I thought, another Remsen Street queer. Sure enough I started seeing him through his open window. The sight lines from our living room window went directly into his apartment. He was literally just a stone's throw away.

I didn't want to actually meet the guy. That would be too direct. I just craved anonymous window sex, good and raunchy. Like in a good porno movie. He seemed interested. It wasn't long before we were into heavy window dressing when our mutual lovers weren't at home. J.O. sex with a kinky edge – he'd strip down nude to just his leather jacket, I'd put on my favorite jock strap and get out the baby oil. One hit from my tiny popper bottle. We were both really into it, posing boldly with no shame. We both liked to shoot our wads into the air. Afterwards, he'd always sign off with a friendly smile. It sure beat J.O. from some dirty magazine. No one could ever see us; it was just our private joy.

Over time I really liked the guy. He was super cute and he knew it in a good way. Up close we'd sometimes pass on Remsen Street. I was strongly tempted to strike up a conversation. Maybe pursue a new lover. He sure was hot. But I'd always stop short. I was too afraid. A sissy. So, no small talk, no introductions, just a big smile and a friendly nod.

21

BARNES CHAPEL AND MARCIA

Marcia was Jim's closest friend when I met him in Ithaca in 1973. She was a brilliant feminist, a Long Island Jew who got her B.A. from Cornell in Feminist, Gender and Sexuality Studies. Before that she'd studied dance in New York City and was in the corp de ballet with the Lar Lubovitch Dance Company for several years. A dance injury was the sudden end of her promising dance career. She returned to Ithaca to heal the psychological wounds. Marcia, Jim and I became best buddies.

Marcia and Jim had their well-established routines. Saturday afternoons they always tuned into the live radio broadcasts from the Metropolitan Opera in New York City. They both knew their opera well. Jim would lip sync with the divas as Marcia cheered him on. Sunday afternoons were reserved for several hours weeding through the Sunday *New York Times*, primarily the Arts and Leisure section. I'd be sure to read the architecture column written by my champion, the *Times* architecture critic Ada Louise Huxtable. She loved New York passionately and wasn't afraid to take on any noble cause celebrating civic life.

Marcia became a gifted writer and landed remote work writing dance reviews for *After Dark*, an entertainment magazine that covered theatre, cinema, stage plays, dance and the ballet. It always featured sexy men inside and on the cover. It had a dedicated gay following; Jim carried a subscription for years. Later on, Marcia ended up as a professor at New York University where she covered the intersection of culture, religion, politics and language. She was an intellectual.

Marcia came out shortly after we met. She had a summer fling with a visiting French lesbian. Florence was employed as a native speaker at Wells College where Jim taught French Literature to the "girls." Jim actually hired her. Florence was terribly French, charming and over-sexed, always on the prowl for pussy sex. She also had a bad case of B.O. which is common throughout France. They don't believe in deodorant. Just splash on some more of that French perfume. Anyway, her academic appointment was for just one year. At the end of it, Marcia was a free woman again and certainly the wiser for it.

Back then I was a photography buff. I had turned our walk-in closet into a darkroom. I'd spend hours walking around outside with my Hasselblad and tripod looking for the perfect moment. I cautiously approached Marcia about doing some dance photos of her. I was afraid it might be too soon. The wound was still fresh. First she declined, but came back a few days later. "How about the solo piece I choreographed for Barber's 'Adagio for Strings?'" "That sounds promising. It will be gorgeous. How about if we use the curved wood stage in Barnes Chapel. It forms a gorgeous brick apse with abstract stained-glass windows. It could be the perfect backdrop for your piece. It's by far the most beautiful space on campus." "You're right Miles. We can use the natural light from the stained-glass windows. I'll wear a plain black draped gown with black shoulder straps." "Marcia, you are going to make us cry."

It was a huge success and we did indeed cry. Marcia was so moving. The black and white photos exceeded our expectations. Marcia's thin, fragile, ivory-colored body was expressive, hesitant, full of heart-breaking anguish. Her gestures to the stained-glass windows formed a link to the divine itself. Barber's slow expressive music fit perfectly. Marcia healed. She was ready to move on.

22

PROMENADE AND FRANCO

It all started when I first moved to Brooklyn Heights before I found a job. With all that free time on my hands, of course I ended up hanging out on the Brooklyn Promenade, cruising. One Tuesday afternoon I spotted Franco in his hot Italian spandex runner's outfit that showed off his butt. Aware of my obvious stare, Franco sat down next to me on the wooden bench. Smiling warmly, then speaking in his adorable broken English, he asked me directly, "Ciao! You horny, si? Want fottere, eh, to fuck bene?"

Unbelievable, you bet I do! Franco was a recent arrival from Italy. He worked for an Italian bank. They put him up in an apartment near the Promenade. Tuesday was his day off. He would get lonely, so he'd come here hoping to get picked up. What luck.

Franco was definitely a "bottom." I could easily understand why given his gorgeous, hairless, smooth-as-a-baby bubble butt. It made me think of Michelangelo's David with his glorious backside in Florence's Accademia that made me almost faint when I first saw it as a student. Well, Franco, my little Italian stud, was the real thing.

After a quick shower back at his place, he settled in on a few giant pillows and soft towels on the floor. He knew exactly what he wanted as he carefully positioned his butt front-and-center, and all for me. I was immediately all over it; Franco moaned for more. I made love for what seemed forever, slapping his butt cheeks until they were rosy red. Then he begged me to butt fuck him. What an honor, yes Sir! Franco and I were in heaven. We were made for each other.

Returning to earth, Franco, with the help of hand gestures, told me to come by the following Tuesday afternoon at two o'clock. He would be waiting for me, all clean on his pillows. He would leave the apartment door unlocked. He handed me a front door key, "You come, si? We fottere, eh, fuck good, bene, bene, eh? "Sure Franco you can count on it". Until I found my job in the city a few months later, I never missed a Tuesday afternoon with dear Franco.

23

INITIATION AND GORDON

Technically speaking, Jim and I lived on Remsen Street in Brooklyn Heights, but whenever we had the opportunity we took the subway over to the West Village. That's where the gays were, no question. The gay bars, the sex shops, the gay restaurants, the gay bookstores. It felt like home. Leathermen strolling down the street together in broad daylight with colored bandanas in their rear pockets, a free hand on your partner's pretty butt. Street hustlers on every corner, just take your pick.

Then there were the gay sex clubs with their backrooms for members only. I'd never been. We'd pass by the solid front black door of the International Stud. Of course, I'd heard about it. As the name implied, it had an international clientele. Wall-to-wall cocksuckers. I was dying to go inside, but Jim would never agree. As if it was too tacky. Like he was somehow superior. I could care less as I noted the address. I knew I'd be back, probably sooner than later, most likely without Jim.

Gordon was Jim's buddy from Princeton. He'd drop by once a year passing thru NYC. Gordon always dressed the part, the olive-green bomber jacket over a white tee, faded jeans, white sneakers. Mr. Sex.

Gordon always liked me. This visit would be special. He was in town to rescue me, to play mentor, the carnival barker, to be my personal guide to the infamous backroom at the International Stud, affectionately known as The Stud. It was cocksucker's heaven. I was thrilled. I couldn't believe Jim went along, like it was no problem.

Why the sudden change of heart? I felt a subtle earthquake. Was I in danger? I didn't really care. I stayed close by Gordon's side.

How did he know I was ripe and ready? That I was meant to pop that night? Ever since the men's locker room at my childhood pool back in Albuquerque I had been waiting for this night. Gordon was wise, especially in matters of sex. He was about to change my life forever. Looking back now, I realize Gordon showed me love, tremendous love, from one gay man to another. He showed me I was not alone, as Sandy had done over a decade before at Camp LaSalle.

As we passed through the black door into the crowded sex den, I felt Gordon's arm on my shoulder like a father's. "You'll be fine Miles. Just relax." Within seconds I was overwhelmed, hit by an incoming tsunami. I was the focus of intense animal desires, half a dozen guys on their knees in the dark patiently taking turns: a hit of poppers up my nose, moist mustaches in my fingertips, yesterday's beard stubble rough against my thighs. In the darkness I caressed his bald head, held his warm ears in my hands, as his powerful tongue pulled me down deeper into his famished throat. This would be my initiation.

24

SEX AND BOMBER JACKETS

Back in those years, everywhere a queer guy turned in New York there was an open invitation for sex. It was exhilarating. Just put on your green bomber jacket, the one with the orange liner. Plus your tightest torn 501 Levi's. Adventure awaits on every street corner.

Here comes another gay bar. Whether you were into leather or chinos, blowjobs or drag, you had your pick. If you were a social misfit afraid to go out, there were plenty of anonymous backrooms, all with the lights turned off. Just grunt and groan to your pleasure. If you're a disco bunny there were a dozen choices, from the high-techno Saint to the low-ethnic Barn, many with inviting sex rooms, for when you need a break from the music. If you are strictly into black leather, head west to the Eagle or the Mine Shaft. Don't forget to bring along some condoms and poppers. If you're a brave pioneer, check out the empty trucks in the Meat Packing District. They're open for full-service all night. If you're the healthy active type of guy, steam rooms like that in the Chelsea offer blowjobs after a good hard work out. Some guys spend days in the baths just fucking their brains out, they like to lose all track of time.

If you're an exhibitionist who prefers the thrill of kinky clandestine sex performed out in the daylight, check out the dilapidated Sex Pier, #52. But you better be super-butch and beware the pier altogether after dark. You could end up a leather corpse in the Hudson.

A bit tamer is the IRT tearoom at Bloomingdales, but make sure you check your shopping bags first. There's always the thrill of a possible New York police raid if you enjoy flirting with a little danger. Sissies looking for a safer pickup, had a wide choice of piano bars, all with plenty of feathers, sequins and colorful drinks. But don't expect to find your Tom of Finland there either. If drag shows are your thing, good luck baby, that's a stage act too hard to follow. No one does karaoke these days, It's considered a little too tacky.

The problem I have with most of these places is that they all take place in the wee hours of the night. I need my beauty rest. I prefer a mid-day quickie at Brooks Brothers in the back dressing cubicle on level two. That, after lunch at the Oyster Bar. Or the well-kept basement tearoom at the Metropolitan Museum of Art, after taking in the Greek male nude sculptures off the main lobby. Our Sunday afternoon piano recital subscriptions at Carnegie Hall always promised a good blowjob from a cute sensitive lad. It's the tearoom off the Dress Circle. Inside it's like Grand Central Station for cultured high-brow fags. There's always a line.

25

CANAL STREET AND MICHAEL

I felt incredibly lucky. I was living alone in the loft near City Hall and I landed a new job at a small hip architectural firm on Canal Street. The office was in the front half of a huge open residential loft belonging to my hippie boss Henry, a super nice straight guy who parked his Harley inside the office. How's that for cool? And get this, Henry's partner Michael was gay.

I had a ball. Lunchtimes I'd rummage through the Canal Street junk shops picking up unusual finds for the loft downtown - industrial light fixtures, steel shelving and steel cable for hanging curtains across the open space. The Canal Street art supply stores gobbled up a third of my salary. I was painting in oil for the first time in my life and I loved it.

Seems like the office mostly did elaborate apartment renovations for rich doctors. They liked my unconventional designs. I proposed a redo for a photographer friend that looked like a giant camera. Michael picked the colors. He really was a color queen. It's a lot harder than you might think.

All things have their season. I lasted a year before moving on to the prestigious corporate architectural firm of Skidmore, Owings and Merrill on upper Park Avenue in Midtown. No more shorts to the office. Brooks Brothers suits were the norm. I didn't mind. I always enjoyed different work situations. It was never boring.

Michael was foxy, but I liked him. He was always putting the make on the gay guys in the office, the two of us. It was the late seventies, the gay party years when guys like Michael went crazy. So I wasn't too surprised when Michael finally made his move. Don't get me wrong, I really liked Michael, as a boss and a friend. He was cool. He seduced me with my eyes wide open. He made it fun for both of us.

Michael suggested we meet early one morning at his apartment before checking out the construction progress at a job site nearby. Great! I had always wanted to see the apartment he had renovated for himself.

Next morning when he opened the door, he was wearing only a skimpy white towel around his trim waist. He chuckled and asked me in. He offered me a coffee. Michael announced he'd be taking a quick shower. "Relax, make yourself at home." Seated in his living room I could easily hear the water running in the shower.

After five minutes, it dawned on me what he was really up to. Sure enough, as I peeked around the corner, I saw Michael inside the glass shower enclosure waiting for me. He smiled, nodding me over with his head. I quickly stripped and joined him. We sudsed up, rubbing each other's chests and backsides, laughing like two kids. He had a great body, nice and muscular. Needless to say we had phenomenal sex and it marked the only time I ever got down on my knees with my boss.

26

TIMES SQUARE AND CALVIN

Did you ever see the 1984 Calvin Klein Underwear Campaign by Bruce Weber? It caused quite the sensation in both straight and gay circles. Huge illuminated billboards started appearing in Times Square and other Mid-town Manhattan sites. Traffic jams occurred, even automobile accidents, as drivers were totally distracted by the hot Brazilian model/athlete Tom Hintnaus shown posing in his Calvin Klein briefs. He's naked except for the brilliant white briefs which pop when seen against his deep tan. He leans back against a white-washed chimney on Santorini Island in Greece with his eyes closed, his hands on his thighs, a sheen coming off his oiled six-pack. There is no doubt the briefs hug a beautiful cock inside. It's definition leaves little to your imagination. He is clearly a sex God.

For the first time in advertising, this iconic image showed the male as sex object. American Photographer named it one of "Ten Pictures that Changed America." I'd have to agree. It updated those boring BVD and Hanes labels that our parent's generation wore. Finally, really sexy revealing underwear to go with our hard-earned gym bods. Sex sells. Four decades later, the label is still an international best seller. Everyone wants to take their turn playing Calvin Klein's sex God. And why not? I like to buy mine at a super slick Italian showroom in Roma's Stazione Termini. When in Rome, do as the Romans do.

27

NYC BALLET AND BOYS

When I met Jim, he was already well into his PhD dissertation from Princeton. It was a long-drawn-out affair, well into its fifth year by the time I arrived on the scene. Jim couldn't have picked a more obscure esoteric topic: the French court ballet during the French Renaissance in the reign of King Louis XIV, the "Sun King." I soon sensed Jim would never complete the ambitious undertaking. For starters, he loathed his thesis advisor. The whole thing sat in an unopened banker's box on the floor in the back of the closet. It concerned me because without his PhD, Jim's future tenure, along with the accompanying job security at Wells College, was unlikely. And where would that leave us?

What is it about gays and the allure of high culture? Doesn't it seem like gays are always more tuned into the arts in general? That was certainly the case with Jim and me. Whether it was Sondheim's "Sweeney Todd" on Broadway, Wagner's "Tristan und Isolde" at the Metropolitan Opera, Balanchine's "Agon" at the New York City Ballet, or Michelangelo's drawings of nudes at the Metropolitan Museum of Art, we were always near the front of the line, the most devoted fans. It's not like we were taught this in school at an early age. Rather it seems like something each one of us had sought out on our own, as if each of us had a deeply rooted connection that required daylight. Or perhaps, it was just an escape into a world we felt more comfortable inhabiting, an addictive fantasy life of beauty and raw sex.

Jim introduced me to the erotic world of the ballet. When I stepped into his apartment that first Spring night after we met, I immediately noticed the striking framed poster for the New York City Ballet hanging over his dining table. It was a prized possession; an abstract design of red, white and blue defining a ballerina on point, it captured the rarified world of the ballet perfectly.

When we moved to New York City a year or so later, Jim would insist we carry season subscriptions each year. I too soon became a devotee of the master choreographer, George Balanchine and his corps de ballet of perfect precision dancers, the otherworldly anorexic women, incredibly thin and delicate, and the sexy athletic young men, erotic in their white tights that showcased tantalizing genitals so clearly. I could easily appreciate why Jim was so interested. It was all so erotic. After taking in an evening of the ballet, all those sexy men in white tights, I'd stand up at intermission with an aching boner in my crotch, only to discover that all the other gay men in the audience were similarly aroused.

At times the ballet really did seem like just a bit of high-brow cultural snobbery, a dressed-up version of the strip-tease act at your local gay club. High culture go-go boys to drool over after your intermission champagne. I'd always replay those almost pornographic tapes in my head of the young male dancer's plump baskets just waiting to be unpacked, those gorgeous firm butts begging to be seduced while keeping time to Tchaikovsky's perfect score. The not-so-subtle sex acts on stage, were thrilling to watch night after night, always the perfect turn-on before a late-night pitstop at The Stud's back room on our way home.

28

BROOKS BROTHERS AND GUISEPPE

Jim introduced me to Brooks Brothers on Madison Avenue in Manhattan. Near Grand Central Station, it was the flagship store dating back to the store's founding in 1818. America's oldest clothier, it was an institution for New York City snobs into penny loafers, chino slacks, button-down Oxford cloth shirts and classic navy blazers. This was for the white Ivy League boys like Jim, the Hamptons beach crowd, those pampered bigots with too much money and too little humanity. It's where Jim and I shopped for our striped silk neck ties, our pink Oxford cloth shirts and our seersucker summer sport coats. I even had a tailored custom-made pin-striped three-piece business suit. I was a Brooks Brother's faggot. Jim taught me how to project the right image, the haughty attitude, the bored expression, the dismissive gesture. "Oh no that won't do, don't you have something a bit more collegiate, you know? Something in Latin with the Harvard seal?"

That first day of spring, I poked into Brooks Brothers over lunch hour to look at the latest summer suits on the second floor; I needed another suit for work. I found the perfect seersucker. In the back fitting room, I stumbled on Giuseppe, a very cute Italian tailor, hanging outside the last dressing cubicle with the curtain half drawn. He was leaning against the back wall with one knee raised. In his mouth was a used wooden match stick he kept playing with, licking it with his fleshy tongue. He saw me staring at him. Then he started playing with his tape measure, rewinding the last foot or so over and over while he rubbed his crotch. He smiled. He disappeared into the dressing cubicle. I followed. Inside he had his boner out. He was brazenly measuring the shaft with his tailor's tape measure, A good seven inches plus, I knelt down without speaking a word and gave him a proper blowjob. Guiseppe was pleased. We traded roles. It all happened so fast. It was certainly my most memorable visit to Brooks Brothers. No attitude, just hot sex. I was out of there in less than twenty minutes.

Back at the office, I mentioned it all to Bob. He said he's had oral sex there more than once as well. Once the cute Black salesman followed him into a cubicle and butt-fucked him while standing up with his trousers on unzipped. Bob said it was tremendous. You'd never figure all this at Brooks Brothers, the exclusive clothier to the Hampton's beautiful people. When I told Abbey, he wasn't in the least bit surprised. He'd heard of plenty of action there as well. Afterall, it's practically a gay institution.

29

MECHANIC'S GARAGE AND FRANCOIS

You never realize how special a place is until it's gone. That was the case with my neighborhood foreign-car mechanic in the West Village. My association started during my first round of working at Richard's. I was the new kid in the office, the goffer. I'd return for round two almost twenty years later as a senior associate. I liked Richard. His work was always unapologetically modern and beautiful. He valued my contribution. He gave me independence.

Richard drove a vintage Bentley back and forth to the Hamptons. It was his pampered baby. Every three months it went in for its regular check-up to Richard's preferred mechanic. Francois's shop was located on a pretty tree-lined block of Tenth Street in the Village. Richard knew I was trustworthy – super neat and careful, so he asked me to take in the Bentley one Thursday morning; just hang out until it was done. I liked the idea; a chance to get out of the office and see Francois.

Francois was the owner and the garage's sole mechanic. He only handled the most exotic foreign cars for a short list of devoted clients. I'd met Francois years ago at the Ramrod on West Street, an afterhours leather bar. He was decked out in leather. He had the most beautiful black skin and perfect white teeth, a movie-star smile. We shared a beer and he invited me over to the shop anytime.

The garage had real curb appeal. On a quiet residential street of traditional brownstones, it somehow fit in perfectly, even though it was the only industrial building, with beautifully detailed clerestory north-facing windows. The column-free interior felt more like a recital hall than a garage with its double-height volume and exposed steel trusses. The huge steel doors on wheels were fire-engine red, the only touch of color in the space. Francois kept the place as neat as a pin, which was partly why Richard chose it. My favorite feature was the huge industrial skylight right in the center which was shaded all summer by towering elm trees. Francois had his workbench directly under it. That's where we'd always hang out with beers, where I'd take in Francois's beautiful smile.

It was late August; a hot and humid Friday afternoon. Those who had summer get-aways were long gone. Francois was in front of his garage on Tenth Street, cruising the rare foot traffic that was left. He was enjoying one of those tiny French cigars. I couldn't help but notice the boner inside his white spandex gym trunks. It was massive. He caught my stare and smiled. "Miles, want to have a little fun on my workbench? I'll lock up. Business is dead." His smile told me what else I needed to know. "Sure, I'm game."

He threw down a few clean work pads on the giant mechanic's workbench, expertly slipped on a condom and positioned me carefully. Then with laser focus, he proceeded to give me the "full service." He was the total gentlemen, always starting off slow with each new position, trying them all out one-by-one, looking for the perfect fit. All sweaty and content, I looked up into the elm trees through the giant skylight. My perfect afternoon with Francois.

30

HELLFIRE
AND NEW YORK'S FINEST

It was my first and only visit. I went alone. The Hellfire was an after-hours S&M sex club in New York's Meat Packing District. I would be a voyeur, perhaps even a player. Who could say? It was all a mystery, surrounded by lust and desire. The door was unmarked, unnamed, just solid black. I was hesitant to open it. Once I did that there was no turning back. Was I really ready? Suddenly, the door opened. A guy was leaving. He nodded with a shy smile. We didn't speak. That was the etiquette. This was a world of gestures, of longing glances, of innuendo.

I took in a deep breath of cold night air and I opened the door. It was much heavier than I expected. Inside was a blue world. It was a small dimly lit room. Everything looked icy blue. The lone guy at the counter handed me a gym basket and a ticket. He didn't say a word. I stripped down to my boots and returned the full basket to the attendant.

The most striking thing was the warm red glow in a corner coming up from the basement level. That's where a tight stairwell took you down into the sex den, the stairwell to hell. The guy at the bottom of the stair was there for the long haul, checking out each new arrival, the size of their cock, the cheeks of their butt, the depth of their lonely sad eyes. Were they even worth going after?

It was a red world of intertwined flesh. Bodies joined to other bodies, one organic whole. The red light was that of a butcher's display case. It made the meat look fresh; the meat arranged in perfect rows. I felt men touching my butt, squeezing it firmly, biting it gently, slapping it hard with bare hands. I retreated to a safe corner, peering out on the sea of flesh. I felt an urge to stay there forever, just watching from the sidelines, absorbed in each performance of sexual pleasure. Men lost in complete abandon, pulled in fluid desire.

Suddenly, a policeman appeared square in front of me decked out in the full uniform complete with the cap and thick bushy moustache. He was definitely one of New York's Finest. Or was he? The uniform was definitely official, but was the guy really a cop? He handcuffed me with my hands behind my back. I liked the fantasy immediately as I focused on his beautiful black moustache in front of my lips. It was extremely bushy, soft and coarse at the same time. I touched it gently with my lips, licking it over and over, kissing each hair with affection, licking them all with my tongue. Each black hair turned wet with my saliva, as I took them into my mouth. We made love inside our mouths, taking turns, exploring wet worlds of tongue and flesh. His thick mustache brushed them all, giving me enormous pleasure. I serviced the moustache one last time, leaving it neat and dry. He unlocked the cuffs and set me free with a firm squeeze on the butt. Our performance over, the cop and I left together in search of a comfortable bed.

31

DUNES AND NAMELESS

There's a beautiful long stretch of deserted beach between Fire Island Pines and Water Island. It was popular with nude gay sunbathers back in the eighties. Couples on towels were tucked away in the sand dunes for privacy. A few didn't mind if you wanted to watch them having sex. They actually welcomed it. Sometimes, if you were lucky, they would ask you to join in.

That's sort of what happened in late September. I stumbled on Nameless. He was special. He was in charge. He knew exactly what he wanted. He set a trap. He grabbed hold of my senses and swallowed me whole and left me nothing. He was a sex machine.

The beach was empty, the ocean was still warm from the summer sun. I was walking solo at the edge of the dunes just in case someone was there waiting, waiting for a kindred spirit to appear, an equally hungry partner for afternoon sex. I thought I was ready.

I was in my white Speedos, sunglasses and red baseball cap. I spotted this short naked guy all alone on a pristine white towel lying on his stomach. First just a foot, then a leg. Then his spectacular butt. The most beautiful perfect butt I'd ever seen. Full, round, plump cheeks with the most alluring butt crack imaginable. I stopped frozen in place, silent, fixated on his white tan line and that amazing butt crack. He had a wrestler's body, nice and chunky. Great back muscles. My eyes kept returning to his butt crack. I imagined making love to him. I couldn't wait to rim him. As I approached from the rear I saw a few unopened condoms and a bottle of Uberlube.

He turned to make eye contact, checking out my Speedos. He smiled, but not a word was spoken, he didn't move an inch. He just lay there waiting patiently. He watched me slip off my Speedos and put on the condom. He finally spoke. "Do me right." I joined him on the towel. First, I gave his gorgeous butt cheeks a long massage, squeezing each half hard with both hands. He started moaning as I slapped his cheeks. He really liked that.

Greasing up, I settled in for a nice slow butt fuck. I could tell he really wanted it rough. I arched my back with each full thrust. I gave him everything I had. Exhausted and sweaty, I collapsed on his back. He turned his head up and smiled. "You did real good." We lay there silently, taking in the rhythm of the breaking waves.

Eventually, I stood up to go, Speedos in hand. I put on my baseball cap, ready to resume my walk to Water Island. One last time, I stared at his beautiful backside, his muscular shoulders, his gorgeous buttocks, his intoxicating butt crack. I noticed a "BB" tattoo on his upper right arm. Finally I spoke to him for the first time. "Thanks BB, be well, you're beautiful."

32

CHRISTOPHER STREET BOOKSHOP AND FRANKLIN

For single gay guys like me, the shop was truly a godsend. It really wasn't a "bookshop." Hardly, it was the hottest gay sex shop in Greenwich Village. Besides the sex toys and porno videos in glass cases upfront, its main attraction was the dimly-lit backroom where guys had casual sex. I'd been there numerous times. It's where I made love to my first leatherman. He was fantastic. Whenever it snowed or rained, the boys poured in from Christopher Street. It was our private playground and it was highly addictive. My heart would start racing just walking past the white front door.

Located at the very end of Christopher Street facing the Hudson, in winter it could be brutally cold. But once inside, things were always hot. From the street you'd never know what went on inside. Straights walked by clueless on their way to the Theatre de Lys next door. That's what I really liked about the place. It was quick and easy. Not like the baths that took up a whole evening. When things clicked at the Christopher, it was thrilling, the most exciting place on earth. That's what I always looked for, the unexpected hookup with a hot sexy guy looking for the same thing I was, a quick trip to the stars.

The bookshop was just a plain white storefront with a solid white door. Inside the owner had installed a classic vintage subway turnstile which you'd pass through as you entered the back room. It always made a wonderful mechanical clicking sound. Sort of like a public announcement. "Hey Boys, check out this one!" It was thrilling! Just the sound made a guy like me hard.

The shop owner Franklin is a beautiful Black man. I met him in my therapy group six months before I found my Abbey. Franklin has had two lives. First, he earned a divinity degree from Yale, became an ordained Unitarian minister and got married with a son. The family lived in India for a decade studying Buddhism before Franklin saw the light and came out big-time in his forties. Now he's a bad ass leatherman, owner of the Christopher Street Bookshop, the hottest gay sex shop in the West Village. In the shop he's always decked out head-to-toe in black leather. Franklin knows everybody; he's super friendly, a really nice guy. I love to visit him in the shop. He likes to show me the more unusual items. He makes me laugh tears. Outside the shop, Franklin's strictly into pressed chinos and Izod sport shirts. At home he keeps his treasured butt boy Anthony, a blond kid half his age. Franklin rescued Anthony from the street hustlers who had their claws in him before Franklin came along. Now he and Anthony live in quiet domestic bliss. It's quite touching, really beautiful. Franklin adores Anthony. Anthony adores Franklin.

33

SKIDMORE, OWINGS AND MERRILL AND SIMON

In the late seventies when the national economy eventually picked up, I left the healthcare firm to join the prestigious corporate architects Skidmore, Owings and Merrill located on upper Park Avenue across from the firm's iconic glass skyscraper Lever House. No question, there were lots of closeted gays there during those years, even a Senior Design Partner. It was widely rumored he hung out in the wee hours of the night at an infamous West Village SandM sex club. In contrast, my immediate supervisor was an amusing screaming queen, loved by all, the firm clown, who greeted everyone with a long warm hug. Even though the firm was strictly Brooks Brothers conservative, it gave welcome shelter to us queers. The late evening hours in the Design Studio witnessed plenty of action in the men's room or even out boldly on the Carrara marble table top in the Partner's private rear conference room. That's where Simon and I first had sex.

It all started innocently enough on a Tuesday morning. I needed to pee badly. I was hanging out at a urinal. Suddenly Simon appeared over my left shoulder and settled into the adjacent stall. He peeked over the partition to check me out. "Hi Miles. What a piece!" He proceeded to drop his chinos while turning away to fully expose his derriere for my benefit. Now that I saw Simon's butt in the raw for the first time, I was completely hooked.

Simon lived in a small Midtown one-bedroom apartment only a block away from the office. It had belonged to his favorite grandfather. Simon invited me over one lunch hour. He wanted to show me his new leather chaps. The Hopperesque interior was decorated in shades of brown, drab to say the least, with a large double-hung window facing a lightwell. Simon didn't even bother to get a curtain. He was certain no one could see in.

He told me he jerked-off every night wearing his Harley leather jacket watching the cum fly through the open window into the lightwell. I asked for a demonstration. "I'd love to Miles. Let's break in those new chaps over my bare butt." We both understood what the other secretly craved: raw, unfiltered anal sex. We named our time together: "The Butt Sessions." Simon was my butt boy; I was his butt-fucker. He made me wear his harness, fuck him in his chaps, cum up his tight ass, jerk-off together into the lightwell. It was raunchy. I always used a condom. Simon liked to surprise me. Our lunchtime sex was never boring.

Months passed. The sex slowly ebbed, the love between us grew. I cherished the time after the sex talking in bed, holding Simon in my arms, his mussed hair in my nose. I'd tickle him, make him laugh, make him show me his boyish smile. By Christmas we both knew it was over. We'd never be live-in lovers. Just lunchtime fuck buddies. That wasn't enough.

Within five years Simon would die of AIDS.

34

CHRISTOPHER STREET AND LONESOME

It's Christmas Eve. Jim is in Iowa for Christmas. I'm alone in New York, horny as hell. I decide to dress for cruising. The usual raunchy look. This time no tee shirt, just my 501s, motorcycle jacket plus a tiny popper bottle and a condom. On the way out I grab my Stetson's cowboy hat for good luck. I take the back stairs to the shortcut onto Ann Street. It's deserted outside. Full moon. Light wet snow is falling. Mild temps. Head to the 7th Avenue Local #1 at Church Street. Lucky, I just caught the incoming train.

Exit at the Christopher Street stop. A couple of swishy queens are exiting ahead of me on the subway platform. One looks back over his shoulder to check me out. Afterwards, he slaps his partner hard on the butt for my benefit. He catches my smile. The fresh night air up at the sidewalk feels good. Sheridan Square is quiet. The strong smell of pine needles hits me. The Christmas tree lot is closing for Christmas Eve. The lot is really picked over. Just the losers are left.

I head down Christopher to the Hudson. I plan to hit the backroom at the popular Christopher Street Bookshop. I like it. It's raunchy. The pair of queens from the subway platform is headed in the same direction and sees me. They slow down. Then I spot a guy ahead all alone in a dimly lit doorway. We make eye contact. He's tall and lanky, wearing chaps. Super-hot. I slow down to a crawl. He has his thumbs in his front pockets. He sure looks like a street hustler, but who knows on Christmas Eve. He even sports the raised knee look and the classic butch mustache.

He sees me start to smile. I stop dead right in front of him and slowly unzip my jacket so he can see my pride and joy in the moonlight, my six-pack. "Nice abs." "Thanks. Those are even nicer chaps. Are you staying warm?" "Let's just say the meat inside is almost ready to eat. Go ahead, give it a feel." "Thanks for the invitation." I move in close so I can give this friendly stud a proper squeeze, followed by a nice slow massage. He's already rock hard. "Want some head?" "Sure. Where do you live?" "A loft by City Hall." "Aren't you a ways from home?" I chuckle and give him my best smile. "You caught me! I'm headed to the Christopher Street Bookshop, to the back room to fuck my brains out with a total stranger. I'm pathetic."

"Well that seems like a real shame Cowboy. I mean, first of all, it's too dark to see your gorgeous abs, second it's smokey and third it's Christmas Eve. Don't you have anybody waiting for you at home to kiss under the mistletoe?" "My boyfriend is in Iowa with his family. He's still in the closet at forty. It's fucked up." "I hear you. How about we hop on my Harley and get warm down at your loft. I'll introduce you to Dick here." "Terrific, but only if you'll promise to butt fuck me with your chaps on." "I think that could easily be arranged. What's your name Cowboy?" "Just call me Lonesome."

35

MEAT PACKING DISTRICT AND TOM

He was clearly visible in the brilliant full moon. I was far west near the Hudson in the Greenwich Village Meat Packing District; it must have been past three. It was dead quiet. Not a soul anywhere, except for Tom.

The lone Biker was posing next to his shiny Harley, his pride and joy. He was leaning back against the rough brick wall of the abandoned four-story triangular building. It was the one with the infamous sex club in the basement. His right knee was raised as he rested his motorcycle boot against the brick wall. He looked tired. It had been a long night. Even at a distance I could make out his handsome boyish face, the perfect white teeth of his slight smile. He was a gentle Biker. His worn black leather motorcycle jacket was slightly shiny in the moonlight. His old leather chaps framed his tattered Levi's. I gave him a warm smile. He nodded me over. I was all his.

We were two hungry outlaws. Our encounter was timeless; it had no boundaries. I was immediately on my knees as if in prayer. It was a carnal script, as old as mankind. My Biker looked up to the heavens for God's blessing. We shared in the rites of adoration, taking turns patiently at the altar. He begged me to let up. I didn't. Exhausted he fell in my arms. Then he slowly backed away. His face glistened in the moonlight. He yielded soft moans of male pleasure.

This is what he really needed. We let go at the same moment. Our seed poured out on the damp ground. We were both wasted.

We enjoyed the moment; the cool night air felt good against my sweaty face. Up close in the moonlight, his face really was extremely handsome and boyish. His teeth were perfect when he smiled. He was my first Biker. He was such a beautiful outlaw. I loved him.

36

THE CLUB AND MILES

I've always been a horny guy, going back to the boy's locker room in junior high. I was a born exhibitionist. I liked to show it off in the boy's shower room. Suds it up and beat off. What a thrill. It's not like I have an enormous cock or anything. It's a little bigger than average, but not nine inches like some lucky Black guys. But it's a good handful. It's beautiful; I'm blessed. I soon discovered it was the perfect size for jerking off out in the open. I pretty much jerked off solo every day after my first wet dream. After coming-out in college I got a little more adventurous and paired off one-on-one with a few guys at Cornell. I really liked that, making a visual connection with some horny stud. But it wasn't until I moved to New York City in the mid-eighties, after I broke up with Jim, that I discovered the real thing at the New York Jocks. The J.O. Club. That was the turning point. Bingo! It was tremendous, as if I'd died and gone to heaven. For a horny guy like me, obsessed with dick, it was really perfect.

I had heard about it through a friend of a friend. It was a for-real New York jerk-off club, for members only, that met every two weeks in somebody's big loft in Soho or Greenwich Village. After my first visit, I turned into a regular. I was hooked; I just couldn't get enough. This was all long before I met Abbey. I was lonely with too much free time on my hands. The club was perfect for me. I never missed a session.

Maybe thirty, forty or fifty guys would show up around seven o'clock. After checking members cards, they'd hand you a clean white trash bag for your jacket and clothes, then take it back with a claim number. Everybody stripped down to our boots only. I wore my black leather motorcycle boots with white athletic socks. They'd hand you a mini white-paper cup partly full of creamy white Crisco, perfect for long periods of jerking off since it never gets tacky like water-based KY. The only strict house rule was jerk-off sex only, no oral or anal sex. The place was well lit, so I could see everything clearly. They'd cover the floors and furniture with huge sheets of clear plastic to protect them from the pools of cum.

Guys would usually walk around solo, cruising each other silently. It was very cinematic. Most of the guys had hot gym bodies. Sometimes a circle jerk would form with half a dozen or more guys going at it together. That scene wasn't for me. I much preferred pairing up with some stud one-on-one. The visual connection was essential. I loved to watch the guy up close, take in his whole body, study his hard cock and watch his particular hand technique. The best guys weren't afraid to flaunt it. If you wanted to, he might even let you work his cock yourself. Or vise-versa. I found the whole scene terribly erotic. Often you could see the city below outside the big windows with regular people walking around, doing regular things, while we were all busy adoring cock. The juxtaposition was a turn-on.

It was like we were some ancient hedonistic Sect, performing age-old rituals. We worshipped the cock. It was beautiful. The club only lasted a year or so before AIDS shut it down. I suspect these days, that clubs like the New York Jocks have vanished altogether. Only old-timers like me remember them fondly.

37

PARADISE AND JAKE

The house had a reputation for queer leather sex. It was always dark and secluded. I liked to take afternoon naps there. I'm not really much of a beach person. That afternoon it was nice and quiet. I had passed out in the nude on the king-size bed in the master bedroom which Abbey and I had for the season. I woke up to muffled sounds of someone moaning. I quickly realized it was Jack and Mike having sex on the other side of the flimsy wood partition. I tip toed to their door in my socks and peaked in through the vertical cracks. Mike was standing upright in a black leather harness while Jake spanked his beautiful bare butt. Jake was using an old black leather paddle. He made loud sharp pops with each firm slap. Mike's butt was a bright rosy red. They didn't see me.

Jake was in his early sixties. He was in great shape, tight and muscular. His voice was deep and sexy. I guess I always looked up to Jake as a father figure. I was fascinated by his butch leatherman's persona. He wasn't a sissy like me. He always wore old leather chaps over Levi's and a simple leather vest over a white tee. He had the classic thick black moustache. He'd see me always staring at him. He'd jokingly ask me if I wanted a spanking. I'd laugh and say "You know I do Daddy. I've been a bad boy."

That Saturday afternoon I was home all alone in the main house. I was curious what sex toys Jake and Mike had stashed away in their bedroom. I was going through the top drawer when suddenly Jake showed up in the doorway. He'd caught me in the act.

"Looks like Miles has been a bad boy. Daddy is going to have to give him a spanking." I smiled. I guess I secretly wanted exactly that. I slipped off my Speedos and turned to face the rough wood wall with my arms fully extended.

Jake first squeezed the tan line on my butt cheeks roughly with his hands. It felt good. Then he slapped the cheeks hard with his large bare hands. Loud sharp pops filled the room. I felt a deep burning sensation. "You need a proper spanking boy." Jake retrieved his leather paddle from the lower drawer, the same paddle I'd seen him use on Mike. Without hesitating a moment he delivered an extra firm slap to my butt, then another and another. Instantly, I felt a deep sharp numbing sensation. I asked for more. The loud pops echoed through my head. It was painful and wonderful at the same time. I felt completely alive, fantastic. I asked for more.

38

PIER 52 AND VOYEURS

I had already visited Pier 52, the infamous clandestine "sex pier." Jim was my initial guide on several occasions years ago, before we split up. But those limited tours of the West Village gay landmark only covered the building's vast crumbling exterior. As two timid voyeurs, we always kept a safe distance, we never dared to venture inside. Rather, we stared up in awe at the shirtless men hanging out at open decayed windows on the upper floors, some walking around nude with semi-erect cocks and most memorable of all, some brazen exhibitionists performing sex acts out in the open for all to see, free of charge.

Now, when I finally returned years later to Pier 52, I was on my own, seeking out a little closure, perhaps even a little adventure. Jim had died of AIDS a year before. I felt his silent approval, urging me on this time around. It was in early Spring, a brilliant clear Sunday afternoon with a cloudless cobalt blue sky. I was hyper-aroused as I saw the enormous hulk of Pier 52 appear through the white blossoms of the flowering pear trees at the end of Gansevoort Street. It still looked spectacular. The same industrial ruin I had first admired years before, still abandoned and dilapidated, its secrets hidden away inside. Its huge rectangular form was still jutting out proudly into the Hudson River, like an enormous pleasure palace. But it was still a shock to rediscover the side view, the massive repetitive form, which had long ago partially collapsed, under its own weight in a fire. A portion had morphed into an enormous wave-like shape near its west end toward the river, its roofline now that of a carnival roller-coaster.

This Sunday I vowed to return and to go inside. It would mark my first and last solo visit. How appropriate that it was a Sunday, for the cavernous interiors had a church-like luminosity. It lived up to its hallowed reputation. Huge interior spaces in total ruin, hushed tones of reverence, dangerous cat walks, men cruising men everywhere, lots of black leather, lots of sex and lots of nudity. At the far west end wall, the urban artist, Gordon Matta-Clark, had made a huge crescent-shaped light-flooded hole in the exterior wall facing the Hudson River. He titled it "Day's End." It formed a perfect church altar. Its brilliant pool of sunlight illuminated the floor of rough timbers. That's where at least half a dozen leather-clad guys were enshrined, performing perfectly each role of a forbidden gay orgy. I and a few others just watched speechless. The performers silently welcomed us onlookers. There was a mutual unspoken trust. The stillness was punctuated by moans of pure pleasure and the loud sharp pops of raw flesh being slapped; it was electric, hot-as-fire, frightening, unbelievable, violent and yes, beautiful.

I studied the sex performers for hours, up close and from a distance. I kept to myself, pure voyeur. This Sunday would be my only visit—I made sure to take in enough to last a lifetime. This brief glimpse into gay heaven and gay hell would be sufficient.

39

THE CHELSEA AND BRIAN

Ordinary people walked by unconscious of the overhead display of queer pride. Only the rhythmic sound of clinking dumbbells and steel plates told you this was the Chelsea Gym. It was in another world. At the corner of 17th Street and Eighth Avenue, it was on the second floor above a video store in an old red brick building. The corner full-height windows went right down to the floor, so from the sidewalk level below, I could look up to see some Adonis in skimpy gym trunks pumping iron. He'd be completely silent as he'd lift a hundred plus pounds of iron like it was nothing. They were all magnificent. I told myself, I was going to look like them one day.

I loved the casual camaraderie, the family atmosphere. When Jim and I split up I finally joined the Chelsea. Jim never understood all the fuss. It belonged to my generation. We needed a butch alternative to the in-your-face drag queens. Between the guys at the free weights and those hanging out in the steam room, I did just fine. I never felt lonely inside the Chelsea. No attitude, just hot guys into muscles, plain and simple. I loved to spot for a shy guy, push him to his limit, watch him smile as I cheered him on for another rep. I'd always congratulate him after a long workout. We'd hit the showers laughing, stretch out on a steam room bench together, maybe trade blowjobs after all that looking. It was a gay man's heaven.

I met Brian on the chest press. He offered to spot me. I was immediately hooked on his cute smile, that and his spandex gym shorts that revealed everything I wanted to know. He'd position his legs snugly around my head as I pressed the barbell up. I practically had his privates in my mouth. We became gym buddies. Every Tuesday and Thursday afternoon at three o'clock we'd meet for a long intense work out, followed by equally intense sex in the steam room. We liked to jerk off together, working each other's piece until we popped the bejesus.

When I finally made it to Rome, I made a point of touring the ancient Baths of Caracalla. This enormous ruin was the predecessor of the modest Chelsea back home. I wanted to experience firsthand the grandeur of its vast vaulted halls filled with ghosts of the past, including those founding emperors, Severus and Caracalla. These guys were never in a hurry, taking their time slowly butt-fucking young athletes out in the open. Their primal moans of sexual pleasure echoed across the vast heated pools. It was an exclusive masculine world, unapologetic, just like the Chelsea, dominated by sexual bravado and pure exhibitionism.

40

SHOWDOWN AND MARSHA P.

Marsha P. was legendary. I'm talking about Marsha P. Johnson, a founding member of the Gay Liberation Front (GLF), co-founder of Street Transvestite Action Revolutionaries (STAR) with Sylvia Rivera. Marsha was also a model for Andy Warhol, an AIDS activist with ACT UP and she was commonly known as the Mayor of Christopher Street. She was tall, slender and fearless, the glamorous saintly queen of "high drag."

It was 1971, within a year of Abbey's coming out and a good decade before we met. It's fair to say Marsha P. saved Abbey's life, or at very least, spared him horrific scars. He was out late doing the after-hours gay club circuit in the West Village. He was just a kid, twenty years old. In New York regular bars closed at two in the morning, but private clubs could stay open much later. West of Christopher Street was where all the hottest clubs for young gays were located. Abbey particularly liked The Barn, a popular after-hours gay club that featured colorful disco dancing upstairs and an infamous back room for sex in the basement. Abbey loved to take his shirt off and work up a sweat, dancing with the young hip gays who formed a closely knit brotherhood. Everybody knew each other. It was that kind of a place. Super friendly.

That fateful night Abbey was coming from the Christopher Street Station on the IRT #1, heading down Christopher Street towards the Hudson River. Passing Bleeker Street, he stayed on the north side of the street. Everything was shuttered up tight. Not a soul anywhere. It was a little too quiet, a bit creepy. Suddenly, he heard distant voices behind him. As they gradually got louder, he could make out distinct words. "Hey faggot. Slow down faggot. We have something to show you. What's the hurry faggot? We're all gonna fuck you. Bet you'd like that faggot." Terrified, his heart racing, Abbey started walking faster, but not running, so as to not provoke them, just walking briskly to keep a distance. He didn't dare look back. He didn't want a confrontation. But he was fully aware that he was only midway down the block, it felt like a mile to safety in The Barn. He dared to steal a quick look back; there were three of them. OMG, two are carrying what look like baseball bats. Their voices were getting even louder. The taunts were even bolder. "Hey faggot boy, time's up. Time to get fucked."

At that exact moment, Abbey heard a deafening explosion of breaking sheet glass, the powerful sound completely filled the empty canyon of Christopher Street, from wall to wall, even up into the heavens. Stunned, Abbey stopped and turned around. He heard the blood curdling shriek of a towering Amazon, "You mother fuckers! You god damned mother fuckers!" An enormous woman was on the opposite sidewalk; she crossed the street in a diagonal line, walking rapidly towards the gang, hurling two more huge glass bottles at them which shattered at their feet. KABOOM! Bam! KABOOM! Bam! Turning around, the cowards fled like frightened rats. Feeling as if he was in a war zone, which in a real sense he was, Abbey walked rapidly west, toward the Hudson, almost running, until he reached the safety of the club. Pausing once to look back, he was looking for the giant woman, but she had vanished.

Years later, he would have a chance to thank her in-person, at a New York Gay Pride Parade. Marsha P. Johnson, much more than a drag queen, she was also the beloved Mayor of Christopher Street. She single-handedly saved my Abbey's life.

41

MANEUVERS AND ABBEY

I met Abbey on Memorial Day weekend, Tuesday June 1, 1982, in the leather bar Maneuvers, in the Meat Packing District. It was two o'clock in the morning on a rainy spring night. The attraction was immediate and overwhelming. Abbey knocked me off my feet. God was he gorgeous. When he spoke my head felt numb. I felt drugged. It was marvelous. I guess you'd say I'd fallen in love in an instant. It was like a fairy tale.

That night we barely spoke. He was with his boyfriend Julian. They were on the verge of breaking up. Their one-year relationship would be over by sunrise. It wasn't my doing; our fortuitous meeting was just by chance. We exchanged phone numbers after the briefest of introductions. I wouldn't see Abbey again until Friday night after work. Meanwhile we'd talk every night on the phone for hours. His deep sexy voice made my head spin. My whole body ached waiting for his phone calls.

When Friday evening rolled around three days later, we exchanged our first kiss. That first night our bodies fit together perfectly. I held Abbey in my arms and kissed his soft warm ears. Somehow, I had found my new beloved. I was the happiest man on earth.

42

VILLA LANTE AND TWO STUDS

Abbey and I were enjoying a long road trip through Tuscany. I wanted to show him the Renaissance water gardens at Villa Lante outside of Viterbo. We parked our rental car in the small visitor's lot off to the side. We noticed steps leading down to an underground public men's toilet. Two vaguely seedy guys standing next to the top of the stair were watching us. They looked like workmen in dirty overalls, maybe masons or gardeners. They were young, in their twenties. Abbey told me they were making him nervous, maybe they were casing our car with its luggage. He wanted to move the car while I took a pee. I agreed and headed toward the steps. As I passed the two workmen they nodded friendly-like. The shorter one gave me a smile.

The underground men's toilet was amazing. It wasn't large, but beautifully finished in small white hexagonal glazed tiles. The antique urinals and sinks were enormous porcelain fixtures with a beautiful crackle glaze finish, nothing like the dinky institutional kind we have back home; these urinals were deep sculptural alcoves that extended all the way down to the floor. A continuous gentle stream of water washed their smooth back surface. A tinkling sound from the gentle cascade filled the room. The most magical feature of all was a large glass block skylight that fractured the sunlight into a thousand shards of brilliant white light. They washed the walls and floor and even filled the huge urinals. My trance was broken by the quiet presence of the shorter workmen. He stopped next to me. He smiled and spoke softly, "Ciao."

Up close I could see he was strong and muscular. He had thick black hair, coarse beard stubble, heavy eyebrows and gorgeous fleshy lips. His olive-colored skin was dusty and slightly shiny in the brilliant light. He was wearing a tiny silver ball earing in one ear. He radiated sex. I realized the two of them were a team, two hot Italian guys looking for action with the tourists. The taller one stayed by the door as a lookout, while the shorter one positioned himself in front of me next to the urinals.

Without the least hesitation, he lowered his work overalls to show me his cock. It was massive, not too long, but nice and thick. He looked like those statues of stocky Roman emperors we had seen in the museum in Rome. I really wanted to suck him off right there on the spot, but he was more interested in my hard-on. He quickly unzipped my shorts taking my cock in his rough workman's hands, rubbing the head hard with a wad of saliva.

I was so hyper-aroused that I exploded almost too quickly, shooting my load into the urinal. He milked my cock, over and over, until the final drop of cum was rinsed away. Completely drained, I turned to touch his thick black hair, perhaps to give him a hug, but he was gone before I knew it. When I returned upstairs, there was no sign of the pair. I had a lot to tell Abbey. But he had already figured it all out, and was patiently waiting for the details. My memories of Villa Lante will always begin in that tearoom with its two horny Italian studs.

43

FOSSE ARDEATINE AND SALVATORE

Few non-Italians have even heard of it. Ironically, that's a blessing. The fact that it's almost always empty, contributes to its aura of healing mystery. I'm talking about Mausoleo delle Fosse Ardeatine, outside the city wall of Rome, near Via Appia Antica, the main ancient road from the south, leading into the heart of the capital. It is the most poignant outdoor memorial I have ever seen. It remains as moving today as when it was completed in 1949.

Fosse Ardeatine marks the sacred ground, of a reprisal killing, during the Nazi occupation of Rome in WWII. The *Blue Guide* to Rome summarizes well the startling bare facts:

> On the 24th of March 1944, after the killing on the previous day of 32 German soldiers by the resistance movement in Via Rasella, the Germans shot 335 Italians. The victims, who had no connection with the incident, included priests, professionals, about a hundred Jews, a dozen foreigners, and a boy of fourteen. The Germans then buried the bodies under an avalanche of sand created by exploding mines. Local inhabitants helped a legal and medical team exhume and identify the bodies after the German retreat. The scene of the massacre, below a huge tufa cliff, now has cave chapels. The victims, now reinterred, are commemorated by a huge single concrete slab placed over their mass grave, with a group of standing figures, in stone, by Francesco Coccia.

The massive bronze entry gate should have prepared me. Its dramatic tangle of twisted bodies, aching for relief, was a clue. The stark perfect carpet of green grass inside was another. The enormous floating horizontal monolith, like a huge sarcophagus lid, which covered the victim's stone coffins, solid and silent. No, nothing prepared me for such a visceral encounter. As I traced the footsteps of the victims to the caves where they were shot, I could hear in my head the pistols firing one-by-one in the back of each victim's neck. The wails.

Later, inside, under the huge concrete sarcophagus lid, with its row after row of identical stone coffins, I realized I was below grade, in their sacred space, still inside the earth where all the killing took place, where they now shared a gruesome brotherhood in death for eternity. The only relief offered them, or me, was a piercing band of blinding heavenly light separating the enormous sarcophagus lid from the sunken earthen grave, only a single foot high, not an earthly window, but the open hand of God himself.

And then I saw the sight that made me weep so freely. Atop each stone coffin, at its center, on its tilted stone lid, was a carved stone laurel wreath, its delicate symmetrical curving branches holding a tiny oval picture frame, like a pair of gentle hands in prayer. Each silver frame contained a black and white photograph of a male victim: bright inquisitive schoolboys, gorgeous young men brimming with life and passion, beneficent priests in their robes with crisp white collars, wise elderly gentlemen with thick beautiful white hair. Each victim's name appeared in front in a bronze plaque. I paused for the longest time at Salvatore, a gorgeous young man with sexy brown eyes, thick black hair and fleshy soft lips. I reached across the stone to kiss his photograph. "Dear Salvatore, you are a beautiful soul, may you rest in peace forever."

I was deeply moved and slightly embarrassed, as if I'd intruded into their silent private world. I turned to leave, feeling relieved, blessed to be joining the living, saying goodbye to the dead before ascending the sunlit stone ramp, which framed a cobalt blue sky and a cluster of giant stone figures looking up to the heavens. I am alive for each of these victims, each of the 335, all beautiful Italian men extinguished in their prime, in the midst of their sweet magnificence.

44

PRIESTLY DRAG AND RODNEY

When we head off to Rome each year for a nice long get-away, I always get an order for priestly drag from my old college classmate Rodney in New York. You see, Rodney grew up in an extremely strict Roman Catholic family in rural Texas. He had a devout set of proper parents and proper parochial schools. You know the story: no meat on Fridays, Confession on Saturdays, Mass and Catechism on Sundays, plus, the cute altar boy thing with that clean crewcut look. Basically, Rodney got the works.

Well, when Rodney finally came out late in junior high, he rebelled big-time and started acting out in healthy ways. First, it was his cowboy phase. He started hanging out around real cowboys. He thought everyone would leave him alone. He got the cowboy shirt with pearlized buttons, the red bandana, the real cowboy boots and even a fancy Stetson's cowboy hat. But he looked awfully prissy when he looked at himself in the full-length mirror in his parent's bedroom. Rodney never dared ride a horse. That was too dangerous. Afterall, Rodney was a sissy. He could never change that fact. So it came as no surprise when the playground bully Doug put an end to all that cowboy glitter. He stripped Rodney down to his BVDs and burned the entire cowboy outfit in a dirt field. He humiliated Rodney. Rodney swore next time he would remake himself in the role model of a strong male figure that commanded full respect like a fireman, a policeman or a priest. He figured no one would dare beat up a priest. He was right. It worked,

Rodney loved playing priest: the black robes, the white collar, the Bishop's hat, the rosary beads, the gold crucifix dangling from his trim waist. Just dressing up as a priest gave him a hard-on. He liked wearing an old ratty jock strap under the robes. He befriended a young priest during confession. After confessing his priestly drag routine the younger priest gladly serviced Rodney in the Vestry after hours. They carried on in secret for years.

Rome has many showrooms for ecclesiastical fashions. It's like Sak's Fifth Avenue for priests. Garments come in a hundred colors, from drabbest brown to papal purple. Anything is possible for a price. Jewels and precious stones are always available. Each piece is a one-of-a-kind work of art. Some outfits are equipped with tiny LED hats for that other-worldly spin. It's a total surround experience. The showrooms often come with piped-in music of heavenly angels. The young salesmen are often quite cute. It seems to attract a cruisey crowd.

45

MADONNA AND ELIO

Pious Mary pondered the busy coffee shop on Arco dei Monti. She saw all who came and went into the shop from her high perch over the square. She missed no one, including the workman Elio who appeared briefly when the shop opened early that morning. He must have felt out of place. He ordered his espresso to go. A water main had broken overnight and the cobblestones needed to be removed before digging a sizable hole to the rupture. Elio was ready in his work boots and orange worker's trousers soiled with mud. His shirt was off exposing his muscular torso. He wielded a giant pickaxe. The work was tedious; he carefully loosened each cobblestone one-by-one with the axe. He was a perfectionist like me.

The narrow street had been reduced to an even narrower walkway tight up against a hastily arranged chain-link fence. That's where I stopped to look at him, his sweaty muscular chest, only a few feet away. He was gorgeous. I smiled and said "Ciao." He blushed. He was so shy. God was he beautiful. "Sei Bellissima!" He smiled for me. I smiled again. "Ciao." I could easily reach out and touch the beads of sweat. Sparkling in the morning sunlight, they ran down his chest from his pecs, across the web of well-defined abdominal muscles into his orange sweat-soaked trousers. He saw my focused stare. He was nervous. He rubbed his crotch for me. I could clearly see his boner. Its massive long shape was clearly outlined by the wet trousers. I tried my best broken Italian. "Let's fuck. Scopiamo, fottiamoli." He blushed red and smiled broadly. "Your Italian is not bad. Yes, yes. Let's fuck."

I motioned with my hand for him to follow me to the toilets. He clearly understood. Once inside we hugged tight. "I'm Miles." "I'm Elio." "Cool name. Sei Bellissima!" Then we took turns jerking each other off like a couple of schoolboys, sucking cock with great gusto, kissing until we were dizzy. Elio was an incredible lover. We shot our loads into the urinal at the same moment. When I started licking his pecs and abs he said "sei, sei." I left beautiful Elio bone dry.

The work crew was done in twenty-four hours. The cobblestones were all neatly back in place by the next morning. Now, every time I pass the coffee shop, I think of Elio, the shy workman with the giant pickaxe.

Mary the Madonna looked down with her beneficent smile. She saw plenty, but she missed the main act. Given the two main characters, she is certain it was most queer, full of lust and desire. She chuckled; a bit jealous. "Those boys sure know how to let loose. I'm trapped up here looking good for the pious pilgrims, while they find forbidden pleasures down there in a tiny men's toilet."

46

LARGO DEI LIBRARI
AND WELCOMES

Our driver Mr. Giovanni dropped us off at Largo dei Librari in front of our mustard-colored apartment building. Everything looked the same as we had left it ten months prior. The school children were still smoking under the white umbrellas at the Tabacchi, the cobblestones were still dusty, but the doll-house façade of our tiny church Santa Barbara looked different. The once gray façade of our charming church had been cleaned to a soft glowing cream in our absence. At eight o'clock the square was already busy. We needed to kill a few hours while waiting for the cleaning crew to finish a pass through of our apartment. No problem, Largo dei Librari felt like our second home.

We decided to have an espresso. We settled in and ordered. Everything was delicious as usual. I glanced at the two middle-aged women at the next table speaking in German quite loudly. Italians rarely, if ever, speak so loudly in public. That's when I noticed that the lady facing me had a remarkable resemblance to our friend Stephanie, our travel companion from last year. What a surprise.

"So you thought you wouldn't have to put up with me this time around, didn't you?" She sounded just like Margaret Hamilton, the Wicked Witch of the West in "The Wizard of Oz."

I bolted out of my chair. I needed to go for a walk. The front door of Santa Barbara beckoned. The door was locked. Churches in Rome open at nine o'clock. I ducked into Da Vinci on the corner, my favorite men's clothing shop in Rome. The sexy clerk Gino will save me. He knows me well. He likes me. Over the years, I'd spent hours in the shop trying on tight-fitting Italian trousers. But no, this morning, only his mother Loretta was in the shop. Gino had to run to Rome's Motor Vehicle Department. I was doomed.

Leaving the shop crestfallen, I rejoined Abbey at our table. Thank God, the pair of German ladies were gone. Their replacements looked like a gay Italian couple in skin-tight jeans and distressed leather jackets. I immediately tuned in with a nod. The cute short one gave me the careful once over with a friendly smile. "Hi, I'm Giuseppe. How's the espresso here?" "Ask my lover Abbey. He drinks the strong stuff. I'm a caffe latte guy. Ciao! I'm Miles. We just arrived." "Welcome to Roma. I'm Piero. Where are you guys staying?" "Right here. The maid is cleaning our apartment. She'll be done by noon." "Cool, maybe we can see more of you guys later." "Just buzz the bell Branzini, any time after two. Maybe you can help us get over our jet lag." Giuseppe smiled immediately. Piero offered to give each of us a massage. I'd say we can count on them for some fun.

Stephanie's ghost witnessed the whole pickup scene. I didn't see her, but I heard her voice clearly inside my head. "You two look like you're up to your old tricks again. Well, play safe. I'll check in later. I miss you."

Four o'clock the door buzzer sounded. I took the elevator down to welcome them in. The tiny cab was packed tight as the three of us headed up. "Sorry, I'm still in my gym clothes. I was unpacking." Actually, I had intentionally put on my favorite jock strap and an old white tank top. Giuseppe noticed. He boldly placed his hand on my butt and gave it a long gentle squeeze. I smiled. Abbey was waiting for us inside in his gym shorts. Piero knelt down immediately without saying a word and started blowing him. I handed Giuseppe a condom. "Go ahead, I think you may need this." We made queer love all afternoon, taking turns trading positions. Horny Piero and Giuseppe welcomed us to Rome. After showers, we shared pizza downstairs in the square.

47

DA VINCI AND GINO

I always keep an eye out for Gino. He looks like a street hustler, with one knee raised leaning against the old stone wall, his hands tucked in his front pockets, a coy smile on his adorable face. "Ciao Miles." Gino is hanging out on Via Giubbonari in front of his shop, Da Vinci, just around the corner from our Rome apartment. "Come inside, I want to show you something." It's noon, Rome's afternoon closing time. After I enter the tiny shop, Gino pulls down the grate and locks the front door. It's a small men's clothing shop, popular for inexpensive sexy Italian men's clothing. I always buy my trousers here from Gino. He knows me well. You can't find pants as sexy as these back in the States. Italian men know how to dress to look really hot.

"How are you Miles? Great to see you again. When these denim skinny jeans came in yesterday, I immediately thought of you. Try on a pair. Here, these will fit you well, just the way you like them." As he hands me the jeans he gives my butt a slap. We've done all this before. "You're right Gino, I need a good spanking. He gives me a couple more, even harder slaps with loud pops. My butt is already turning rosy red.

As I slip on the jeans, I can feel the super-tight fit around my ass, like I was poured into them. Gino slides his hand inside the back of the jeans and rubs my burning butt. "So you like that, my little butt boy." "Yes I do. It feels great. Go ahead Gino. Show me your beautiful Italian cock." This is exactly what Gino planned to do when he invited me into his shop and locked the door. He's done all this a half dozen times before. I'm being manhandled by my favorite Italian stud. After a nice long session, we are both wasted. Gino is dripping sweat.

He hands me the pair of skinny jeans. "These have your name on them. No charge. Thanks Miles. You're always the best. Feel free to stop by the shop at noon anytime. I'm always ready."

48

UFFIZI AND SEBASTIAN

It's the storehouse to the greatest collection of paintings in the world. Caravaggio, Titian, Botticelli, Michelangelo, Giorgione, Tintoretto and so much more. Paintings I dream about, that I carry around with me in my head all day, making love to them, talking to them, holding them in my arms. I am caught up in their stories, I feel their tension, their dreamy repose, their excited anticipation. I weep with them, laugh with them, share a dirty joke with them. When one is missing, reduced to just a tag on a blank wall, I am always crestfallen, like the news of a friend's sudden death. I'll go back next year looking for it, to get reacquainted, to reclaim our kinship. We reconnect. I feel their love across the centuries. It's as real as ever.

Art historians consider him the world's first gay icon. Strong, shirtless, athletic. Tortured, persecuted, suffering. Desired, erotic, resilient. The perfect poster boy for homosexual desire. He's always shown alone tied to a tree with those arrows in his gorgeous body. No angels to help here. He's the martyr, the tough sissy, the anxious closet queen, the exhausted street hustler after a busy night of rough business.

I always look for his painting in Roman Catholic churches. He's never on the main altar, that would cause a scandal, but sometimes he's found in a dimly-lit side chapel, looking down on me with empathy and love. We bond instantly. I want to comfort him; Sebastian and all the other gay men who are alone and tortured. He's our saint, our protector.

There is an exceptional painting of queer Saint Sebastian in the Uffizi by Roberti. He's my favorite Sebastian. A naked muscular athlete in a loincloth. His perfect pecs and abs easily arouse me. He's gorgeous. His ankles are tied together with a thin black leather band. He's bent over a bit, as if wincing from a punch in the gut. Only two arrows pierce his perfect hairless skin—one superficially in his right calf, the other dead on into his bicep. Tight black leather bands strapped to each muscular bicep give him the distinct butch look of a West Village leatherman. He's in rapturous pain.

But it's his troubled facial expression that really gets to me. He shows us his humanity. His head is turned away slightly to the right, as if he feels threatened. Only his left eye is visible. He's staring intensely out of the corner of that eye directly at me, just at me. It's unsettling; but his message is crystal clear. "See me? I'm you. You're me. Do you understand? We are the same."

49

SANTA BARBARA AND FATHER JEROME

I had a thing for young priests while growing up as a closeted queer adolescent in Albuquerque. It never went anywhere really, but whenever I was in our church, the Thomas Aquinas Newman Center on the University of New Mexico campus, I'd always zero in on a handsome tall priest in his long black robes. He was my secret obsession. I never knew his name. We hardly spoke. Our eyes would sometimes meet sharing the faintest smile, grasping for some long-gone connection. Once, we actually crossed paths during Saturday Confession. He was my confessor, seated behind the little sliding screen. I could see his face clearly. It was only a foot away. I confessed my queer sins to him. "I touched myself Father. Many times over. I can't help myself. It was fantastic." He blushed beet red. "And what else my Son?" I didn't have to answer. I knew then, he loved me. He didn't lecture me. He just gave me a light penance of five Our Father's. He skipped the Hail Mary's all together. At my parting, he smiled and whispered gently, "Go in Peace my Son."

Each Sunday at Mass I'd study his gentle face, his sad eyes, his long pale fingers, his beaded rosary tied round his trim waist, the silver crucifix dangling back and forth as he walked past me in the processional. I'd look for signs of his hidden cock, tucked between the thick folds, rubbing up against the soft fabric. He caught me staring and blushed again. The more I watched him, the more I lusted after his hidden flesh, his butt crack, his genitals. He was driving me mad, but I was spared a meeting. I was off to college within a week. Safely across the country at Cornell University in Upstate New York. Only years later would I think back on my childhood crush. During a month-long vacation in Rome, I would revisit my fantasy of making love to a Roman Catholic priest.

The church was tiny Santa Barbara on Largo dei Librai. Our Rome apartment overlooked the pretty little square. I had often ducked inside the church for a brief respite. It was so peaceful. Just inside the dimly lit interior a large tryptic always greeted me—the Madonna and Child, flanked by John the Baptist and a youthful Archangel Michael. The only occupant this day, as was the case most days, was the handsome young priest, the sole caretaker, who was busy arranging the altar with its flowers and candles. We both recognized each other from my frequent visits. But that day his gaze was bolder, less hesitant, clearly more deliberate. I returned his stare. He nodded slightly. I returned the nod with the hint of a smile. I realized it was noon, which meant it was closing time for Rome's afternoon siesta. The priest crossed the small church nave to lock the front door, first pausing to see if I chose to go or stay. That was easy; I remained seated. He looked relieved.

I was quickly aroused. My heart was pounding. He walked to the tall open door of the vestry, turning to see if I'd follow him, which of course I did. High above us were two square paned windows. Brilliant sunbeams illuminated the polished stone floor.

The priest stood so that his black robes were flooded with sunlight. We didn't speak a word. He opened his robes revealing a simple white shirt and soft black trousers. He remained perfectly still as I placed my open hand on his crotch. Clearly approving, he placed his own hand over mine, squeezing it tight so I could feel his cock swell.

Loosening the trouser drawstring, I lowered the soft fabric to reveal his white undergarments. The tight lacing outlined a long soft bulge. Slowly pulling the lacing apart, I finally held his warm cock in my hands. It was perfection.

I knelt on my knees in adoration. My visitation was purely carnal, adoring a priest's perfect sex organ—kissing, licking, sucking it, over and over, my nose in his sweaty crotch. He indulged me, letting me make love to my heart's content in the still sunlight. I lost all track of time. His moans slowly grew louder; our movements more deliberate until we climaxed in heaven. I savored each drop, licking him spotless, kissing the softening cock in final adoration.

Standing up, we embraced once more in the sunlight, my arms engulfing him, my nose in his thick hair, a final languid kiss. He gave me a blessing as I turned to leave. The ancient ritual was complete. He was my first Catholic priest lover, a distant brother from my childhood. As we headed to the front door, we passed a side chapel with a giant fourteenth-century wooden crucifix holding the limp body of Christ looking down at us. Christ's expression was loving, accepting of his own inevitable fate, nonjudgmental of ours, blessing our tender queerness.

50

FREEDOM

This is where I disappear. Where we enter heaven. My eyes are half closed. I'm holding on to Abbey. He's in front of me, driving the Harley. He just washed it. It's spotless, shiny black with lots of chrome, the deluxe model with the big black tires. It rides smooth as a Cadillac. Abbey's wearing my motorcycle jacket and my helmet, the worn black leather jacket we found in Rome over twenty years ago. The front of the jacket is unzipped so I can slide a hand inside and feel his soft hairy chest. It's warm. Abbey is the love of my life.

Abbey is holding Molly in his right hand, her striped paws wrapped around his fingers. She's no trouble. She was never any trouble at all. She's purring loud, as loud as the Harley and as smooth. She's been waiting patiently for a very long time. Her eyes are half closed like mine.

It's dusk, just barely light out. The sky belongs to Turner, or perhaps to Tiepolo. It's God's canvas; it's big enough for both of them. It's pink, turning palest coral and robin egg blue. The night air is cool. I'm in my favorite white tee, the tight-fitting Calvin Klein, and of course my beloved 501s, my second skin, the outfit I liked to cruise in. How fitting for this moment. Abbey and I always ride like this after making love somewhere secluded in a grove of Cyprus trees or on the rocky shoreline at Big Sur. The wind is in my hair. I'm keeping it long again, like in those early days back at Cornell, shoulder length, like Peter Fonda in "Easy Rider." God, he was a beautiful man. There were so many beautiful men on Fire Island.

This is the best part, where we suddenly round a corner and there in front of us is the magnificent Golden Gate Bridge with San Francisco in the distance. It's red-orange art deco steel piers pick up the first rays of morning's pure sunlight as Aaron's "Fanfare for the Common Man" gently greets us. Perfection. Our dearest old friends Jim and Philip are with us, along with Rich and Bob, each couple on their own shiny black Harley, riding abreast, a trio of leathermen. I hear their gay laughter. Thank you God.

Yes, this is where I disappear. Where we all enter heaven. My eyes are closed. I'm holding on to Abbey. He's in front of me, driving the Harley. We are flying. It's spectacular.

www.ingramcontent.com/pod-product-compliance
Lightning Source LLC
Chambersburg PA
CBHW011319070726
47496CB00020B/3022